# CASPER CANDLEWACKS
## in the
## CLAWS of CRIME!

First published in Great Britain by HarperCollins Children's Books 2012
HarperCollins Children's Books is a division of HarperCollinsPublishers Ltd,
77-85 Fulham Palace Road, Hammersmith, London W6 8JB

Visit us on the web at
www.harpercollins.co.uk

1

CASPER CANDLEWACKS IN THE CLAWS OF CRIME!
Text copyright © Ivan Brett 2012
Illustrations copyright © Hannah Shaw 2012

Ivan Brett and Hannah Shaw assert the moral right to be identified as the author
and illustrator of this work.

ISBN 978-0-00-741157-3

Printed and bound in England by
Clays Ltd, St Ives plc

**MIX**
Paper from
responsible sources
**FSC® C007454**

FSC is a non-profit international organisation established to promote the
responsible management of the world's forests. Products carrying the FSC
label are independently certified to assure consumers that they come
from forests that are managed to meet the social, economic and
ecological needs of present and future generations.

Find out more about HarperCollins and the environment at
**www.harpercollins.co.uk/green**

# CASPER CANDLEWACKS
## in the
## CLAWS of CRIME!

Ivan Brett

Illustrated by Hannah Shaw

HarperCollins *Children's Books*

**More adventures with**

Casper Candlewacks in Death by Pigeon!

*For Zanzibar, my bell-ringing cat.*

# Prologue

Deep in the English countryside, in the peaceful valley of the river Kobb, lies a little village called Corne-on-the-Kobb. At first sight its pretty thatched cottages, winding lanes and quaint little cobbled square are no different from any other. But there's something different about Corne-on-the-Kobb; something so wonderfully, uniquely different that someone should write a book about it. You see, Corne-on-the-Kobb is packed full of idiots.

The residents of Corne-on-the-Kobb would lose out in an IQ test against a mouldy peanut. They struggle to count to two, they howl at the moon, some of them have their names and addresses tattooed on their foreheads in case they wander off and need driving home. There are idiots in every home, idiots roaming the streets and an idiot pulling pints at the local pub. Corne-on-the-Kobb is so full of idiots that the government has declared it an area of outstanding natural stupidity and stopped sending it money or biscuits.

However, this story isn't just about idiots. It's also about bejewelled swords and cat burglars and boiled eggs and a boy who lives among the idiots, but forgot to be an idiot himself. But we'll get to him. He's in bed at the moment.

## Chapter 1

# Thief in the Night

Midnight. Time for lunch. In a dusty candlelit room with a sagging ceiling, a wrinkled old woman reached into her plastic bag and pulled out something squidgy wrapped in newspaper. She wore a duffel coat with a woolly tea cosy on her head and thick red lipstick plastered all round her mouth. There she sat, alone in her wheelchair in the centre of the room, smacking her withered lips at the package in her hands. The old woman clawed the newspaper open, feasting her eyes on the oozing corned beef and jellybean sandwich within. One gleeful chomp with her toothless gums sent the meaty gunk splurging all over her trembling fingers and down the front of her duffel coat.

Torn shreds of newspaper drifted, forgotten, to the floor. '*LE CHAT STRIKES AGA—*' said half of the ripped headline. More half-words and phrases settled on top: '*—nother robbery…*' '*… cat burgl—*' '*—ver the head with a cricket b—*' '*—ed by a single cat's whisker…*' But the old woman couldn't give a monkey's armband. She only used the paper to wrap up her sandwiches.

Betty Woons was old. Really, really old. She was so old that barnacles lived between her toes and her wrinkles were protected by the National Trust. She was old enough to be your grandmother's grandmother's grandmother's... well, you get the point.

But Old Father Time had a bit of a job catching up with Betty. She spent her years zipping around the village on her turbo-powered electric wheelchair, knocking over unsuspecting villagers and doing flips off street corners.

Tonight Betty was on guard duty. Behind her, propped up in a smudgy glass cabinet, was the reason she was there: an ancient iron sword dripping from tip to hilt with dazzling rubies and sapphires. The priceless sword had once belonged to the statue of village founder Sir Gossamer D'Glaze in the Corne-on-the-Kobb village square. But two months ago, during what is now referred

to in trembling tones as 'The Donkey Disaster',
the statue was destroyed. Ever since that day the
villagers of Corne-on-the-Kobb had been taking it
in turns to watch over Sir Gossamer's bejewelled

sword, give it a daily jewel massage and read it a
bedtime story.

Betty yawned and slurped the final chunks of
jellybean from her gums. She hadn't a clue why
the old sword needed guarding anyway. Granted
it had been a glorious trophy hundreds of
years ago, but now half the rubies had fallen
off and the end was chipped. Betty had
been using it as a back scratcher for the
past two months when nobody was looking.

There was a rapid knock at the vault door.
Betty's wrinkles wrinkled in wonder. Who could
it be at this time of night? Nobody came knocking
in Corne-on-the-Kobb in the middle of the night
unless they were sleepwalking or they'd lost their
house. Perplexed, Betty squeaked her wheelchair
over to the door and pulled it open.

"Oh," she croaked, "Hello, dear. What brings you out at this time of night?"

There was no answer, just a swift flash of white wood as the cricket bat swung down and spanked Betty on the top of her head. With a pitiful whimper she crumpled to the stone floor like a soggy bag of spuds.

The alarm didn't wake Mayor Rattsbulge at first; he just wiped the dribble off his chin, grunted and rolled over. He was having a cracking dream about hog roasts, and really didn't want to wake up before he'd reached the apple sauce. But then the noise seeped through the non-food part of his brain (a tiny section squeezed away behind the *locum hamburgarium*) and he leapt out of bed as if he was covered in bees. He threw on his extra-large dressing gown and blundered out of his extra-large bedroom on to the pitch-black landing, tripping over the banister and tumbling down the stairs. He bounced at the bottom (thanks to his six bowls of jelly for pudding) and landed rather gracefully on his blubbery feet. Mayor Rattsbulge rushed out of the front door, stopping only to grab a Cumberland sausage from the jar on the hall table. It took him a good three minutes to heave himself to the other side of the lamplit village square, where a small crowd of villagers in their pyjamas had gathered by the door to the village vault.

Audrey Snugglepuss, loud-mouthed village gossip and baker of cakes, strode forward angrily and flicked her nightcap out of her face. "For crying out loud, Mayor Rattsbulge, I'm trying to sleep," she warbled.

"Here here," sang Clemmie Answorth, a slightly younger, nervous-looking woman, completely peppered with bruises and still clutching her teddy. "What with all that racket, I fell out of my bed." She did that a lot.

Mayor Rattsbulge wheezed and clutched his chest. "Ladies, please." He leant on a lamp-post, but it buckled under his weight. "I've only just got here. Now, what's the alarm?"

Mitch McMassive, the tiny landlord of the village pub The Horse and Horse, stuck his little hand in the air and squeaked, "Look, mayor." He trotted forward to the heavy wooden door and gave its brass handle an almighty shove. It groaned open groggily on its rusty hinges.

The bolder villagers bundled through the door into the blackness, and tripped straight over an empty wheelchair. Clemmie Answorth screeched and tinkled through a glass cabinet, while all around dull thuds told stories of foreheads meeting walls and coming off the worse.

Audrey Snugglepuss fumbled for a light switch in the dark. Her first attempt found Mitch McMassive's button nose, which snicked smartly out of joint and failed to make the room any lighter. She finally found the switch and the vault was plunged into dazzling amber light.

"My nose!" honked Mitch McMassive, through

a crimson torrent running down his face. "I can smell blood!"

Betty Woons blinked awake and chuckled at all of the bodies rolling around her. "Oh, hello, dears," she warbled. "What are we all doing on the floor? Sleepover, is it?"

Mayor Rattsbulge was the first to notice. "Oh, my sweet Lord…" he whispered, prodding a trembling finger towards the cabinet. "It's… gone…"

Clemmie Answorth spluttered. "The sword's gone?"

"Who used it last?"

"Well, I didn't take it," said Audrey Snugglepuss.

"What about my nose?" squeaked Mitch McMassive.

"SHUT UP!" bellowed the mayor. "Shut up and find it. Find my sword!"

The pyjama-clad crowd screamed and ran out into the moonlit square, searching under doormats and tipping over flowerpots. Meanwhile, back in the vault, village gardener Sandy Landscape (who'd watched *three whole* detective shows on telly so he knew what he was talking about) edged closer to the cabinet. "'Ere… mayor…"

"What is it?" sobbed Mayor Rattsbulge from behind his gravy-stained hanky.

"I found me summink. Look yer eyes on that." Sandy's grubby fingers reached into the cabinet and pulled out something black and wiry. He held it to the light, and gasped.

It was a single cat's whisker.

## Chapter 2

# Heaven-Scent

"What is your name?"

"Casper Candlewacks."

"How old are you?"

"Eleven."

"What is your favourite flavour of ice cream?"

Casper gritted his teeth and winced. "Mushroom ripple?"

KABOOM.

Clods of scorched yolk exploded over the

garage, covering Casper, Lamp and every exposed

garage surface in a stinking slimy film of egg.

"It worked!" cried Lamp.

Casper smeared the eggy grot from his face and

grimaced. "Sort of…"

"Too powerful?"

"Too powerful."

Lamp Flannigan scratched his chimney-brush hair, pulled a spanner from his boiler suit and set to work adjusting a nut deep inside the contraption.

As his friend tinkered away, Casper Candlewacks sat down on the floor and grinned to himself. Out of all the things to do on a baking hot August afternoon, he could think of nothing better than sitting in his best friend's grimy garage, working on their latest invention and blasting a few dozen eggs to a few dozen smithereens. Casper had spent most of his summer in Lamp's garage. It's not that he didn't like his own house, but things had got a little hectic recently.

Casper was a blonde-haired, keen-eyed scruffbag of an eleven-year-old. He didn't have any superpowers, he hadn't been to space and he'd not even slain a single vampire. In fact, until two months ago, Casper's life was about as exciting as a six-hour guided tour of the Kobb Valley carrier bag factory and shop (where you can buy all the carrier bags you want, but they never have anything to put them in). But then he poisoned a magician, got his village cursed, got attacked by  a flock of man-pecking pigeons, survived a high-speed road accident, swam through a sea of bubbles, destroyed a coriander festival and rode home on the back of a Shetland pony just in time to save his dad from certain death. (Apparently there's a really good book about it too, but I haven't read it.) You'd think that such heroic actions from such an ordinary boy would be rewarded with a medal, a national holiday or at least a pat on the back and a flapjack, but no, no, and one for luck – no. The idiots of Corne-on-the-Kobb ignored Casper Candlewacks like a bad smell in a lift. *He* could do brainy things like reading and writing; *he* could tie his own shoelaces and walk in straight lines. These things were beyond Corne-on-the-Kobb's villagers, so they resented Casper and pretended he didn't exist.

"Any more eggs?" asked Lamp.

"Loads."

The latest additions to Lamp's garage were Mavis and Bessie, two prize egg-laying hens. They had arrived unannounced at the front door two weeks ago, carrying little suitcases and claiming to be distant relatives. Lamp's mum let them stay. All day long they strutted around eating grain, pecking visitors and laying dozens upon dozens of eggs. In fact, they laid so many eggs that every one of Lamp's inventions  over the last fortnight had involved the blasted things – be it the remote-controlled bacon detector or the hover-omelette.

If you hadn't guessed, Lamp Flannigan was an inventor. He was also a short, podgy boy with a scrub of soot-black hair and a dongle of a nose that would be a fantastic door knocker, if it wasn't made of skin and currently attached to a face. Lamp was an idiot too, but he wasn't like any other idiot you'll ever meet. His idiocy went off the scale, went all the way round and came out on the other end. Lamp thought in ways that normal people couldn't (Casper suspected Lamp's brain was made out of a substance not unlike fizzy mashed potato), so he spent his time building things:

amazing, inexplicable things that you'd probably call impossible. Two months ago he'd driven Casper to Upper Crustenbury on a buggy that ran on washing-up liquid. Today, he was inventing a lie detector that used the power of dishonesty to boil an egg. It turns out, Casper had discovered, that inventing egg-boiling lie detectors is a messy old process.

*KABOOM!* Another egg-splosion rocked the garage, exuding a cloud of stinking yellow smoke that insulted Casper's nostrils and sent Mavis and Bessie squawking back into their coop and slamming the door.

"Hello," a mystery voice said.

Casper shrieked and whisked round, but the egg smog was thick and he couldn't see a thing. "Who's that?"

"My name's Daisy," the voice said. "Pleased to meet you."

As the fug settled, Casper began to make out the shape of a girl, about his height, standing at the entrance to the garage. She had brown curly hair, big green eyes and the most beautiful smile Casper had ever seen. She wore a flowery green frock with a ribbon in the middle.

Mavis and Bessie poked their beaks out of the coop and clucked jealously at the intruder.

"What on earth are you doing?" The girl called Daisy looked round at the eggy mess of a garage and then pulled a face at Casper.

"We… uh…"

Lamp's mouth was hanging open. He wiped the egg from his eyes and blinked. Then he shook his head and wiped his eyes again, but that just spread

the egg back on. "Casper," he whispered, "is she real?"

Casper jabbed an elbow into Lamp's side. "I'm Casper," he said to the visitor, "and he's Lamp."

"Did we make her?" Lamp eyed the lie detector with a face of complete bemusement and twiddled a knob on the side. "It's not s'posed to do that," he mumbled.

Daisy chuckled. "We only moved in a couple of weeks ago. I live down the road." She trotted into the garage and picked up a clipboard, upon which Lamp had drawn a diagram of an egg, with labels pointing to its brain, spleen and vocal cords. Then she spotted the lie detector. Inside a large steel saucepan sat the engine from a leaf-blower, grumbling busily, turning oily cogs and rusty axles, all set round a small china dish in the middle

to hold the egg. A trigger had been welded to the handle, and an antenna with a green golf visor poked out above the pan, rotating and beeping mechanically. "What's that?"

"Do you like it?" asked Lamp, blushing.

"Well, I…"

"You can have it if you want." He picked it up and handed it to Daisy.

"I don't really…"

"Come on, Lamp," said Casper. "Put it down."

Lamp sniffed and plonked the pan back on the table.

By now the hens had emerged and were pecking at Daisy's ankles.

"It's a lie detector," said Casper. "Lamp's an inventor."

Lamp grinned at Daisy. "An inventor means you invent things." He pointed at his watch, which was made of chocolate. (It tells you when it's time to eat it.)

"Does it work?" asked Daisy, motioning to the lie detector.

"Sort of," said Casper. He remembered that he

was covered in egg and blushed.

A female voice floated in from outside. "Daisy, darling?"

"That's my mum," said Daisy. Then she called, "Mum, in here. I've made some friends."

Round the corner swept a tall, glamorous woman with the same curly brown hair and bright green eyes, wearing a flowing blue dress and a floral brooch. She flashed a ravishing smile, the sort of smile that would melt the heart of even the frostiest snowman.

Lamp fell over.

"Hello," she said. Her voice was cool and refreshing. "I'm Lavender. Lavender Blossom." She reached out her hand, which Casper shook despite the egginess of his own. "You've met my daughter Daisy."

"H-hello," Casper stammered. They'd never allowed females in the garage, let alone beautiful ones, and this was exactly why. What were you supposed to do with them? He thought about offering his guests a seat or a cup of tea, but the garage didn't have either. Lamp, crimson-cheeked and breathless, took one more look at the visitors and then scrabbled away on all fours to the back of the garage to tinker about with a driveshaft.

"Do you want some help?" asked Daisy. "I'm good at—"

"Now, now, Daisy," Lavender interrupted. "We don't want to interfere." She placed her hand on Daisy's shoulder and smiled gently at Casper.

"So… um… what brings you to Corne-on-the-Kobb?" said Casper, relieved to have thought of something to say.

"We own the flower shop," Daisy chirped.

"Flower shop?" Casper laughed.

"Yeah."

Lavender looked ruffled. "We opened two weeks ago."

"Really? In Corne-on-the-Kobb?"

Lavender reached into her dress pocket, pulled out a little flowery business card and handed it to Casper. It read:

*Blossom's Bloomers*
*'They're Heaven-Scent.'*
*Visit us on the corner of the village square,*
*next to the sweet shop.*

Casper nodded and stuffed the business card into his pocket. "Sorry, I hadn't heard of you. We spend a lot of time in this garage, don't we, Lamp?"

Lamp squeaked.

"That's OK," said Lavender. "Drop in if you're passing. We've got a summer sale on."

"If you buy a full bunch, you'll save a whole bunch!" sang Daisy.

"Sounds good. I'll… um… definitely buy a full bunch then."

"Will you? That's brilliant!" Daisy skipped forward and planted a kiss on Casper's cheek.

"Right then, darling, plenty more of those cards to hand out before tea time." Lavender wrinkled her nose cheekily at the boys and sauntered out of the garage.

Daisy skipped into the sunshine in pursuit of her mother, stopping to chirp, "Nice to meet you," before disappearing round the corner.

The garage was quiet again. Lamp shuffled towards Casper with a worried sort of face on. "Casper?"

"Yes?"

"I can't feel my feet and my heart's gone thumpy. What's wrong with me?"

"I think you're in love, Lamp."

"Oh…" Lamp mouthed the word 'love' to himself a few times, and then wrote it down on his clipboard. "Is that bad?"

"I don't really know," said Casper. "I hope not."

The boys worked in silence for about an hour and a half, disturbed only by the occasional clink of cogs or the whirr and crackle of Lamp's hamster running furiously on its electric wheel. But gradually another noise swelled in the distance, a mix of yelling and clanging and stamping of feet.

As the sound grew louder, Casper could make out the frantic ringing of a bell and the screams of a lady who must have been either very upset about something or a terrible singer. The boys scurried outside and were presented with the sight of that nervous wreck Clemmie Answorth tearing down the road at full speed, swinging a bell precariously round her head.

"HEAR YE," she screamed. "HEAR YE!"

Casper and Lamp leapt back as Clemmie thundered straight past them, clanging her bell in their faces as she passed. She reached the end of the street, tripped over, sprang to her feet and raced back again. More villagers had appeared at their front doors now.

"I SAID, HEAR YE!" There was a rip in Clemmie's skirt and she was missing a shoe. "MAYOR RATTSBULGE…" – she was quite out of breath – "REQUIRES YOUR PRESENCE… Oh, dear." Sandy Landscape gave her a full watering can and she drank gratefully. "Thank you. IN THE VILLAGE SQUARE, AT ONCE!"

She dropped the bell, chased it down again and clanged off in the direction she'd come from.

"Ooh, are we getting presents?" Lamp's face perked up.

"No, she said 'presence'. We're meant to go to the village square."

"Not even one little present?"

"Perhaps something even better, Lamp." Casper felt a surge of excitement like he'd not felt for exactly two months. "Let's go and have a look," he said. And so they did.

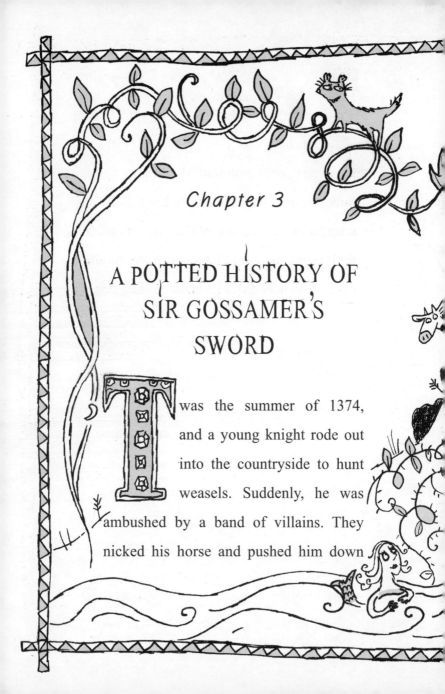

# Chapter 3

# A POTTED HISTORY OF SIR GOSSAMER'S SWORD

**T**was the summer of 1374, and a young knight rode out into the countryside to hunt weasels. Suddenly, he was ambushed by a band of villains. They nicked his horse and pushed him down

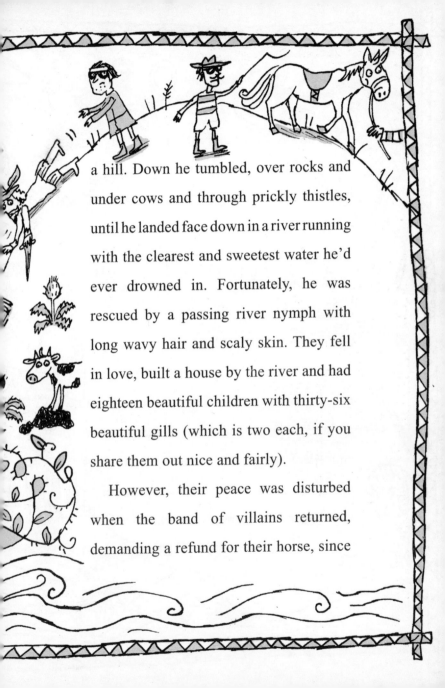

a hill. Down he tumbled, over rocks and under cows and through prickly thistles, until he landed face down in a river running with the clearest and sweetest water he'd ever drowned in. Fortunately, he was rescued by a passing river nymph with long wavy hair and scaly skin. They fell in love, built a house by the river and had eighteen beautiful children with thirty-six beautiful gills (which is two each, if you share them out nice and fairly).

However, their peace was disturbed when the band of villains returned, demanding a refund for their horse, since

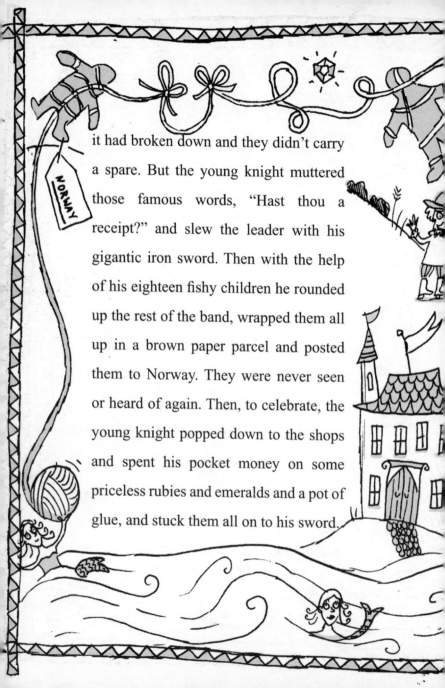

it had broken down and they didn't carry a spare. But the young knight muttered those famous words, "Hast thou a receipt?" and slew the leader with his gigantic iron sword. Then with the help of his eighteen fishy children he rounded up the rest of the band, wrapped them all up in a brown paper parcel and posted them to Norway. They were never seen or heard of again. Then, to celebrate, the young knight popped down to the shops and spent his pocket money on some priceless rubies and emeralds and a pot of glue, and stuck them all on to his sword.

NORWAY

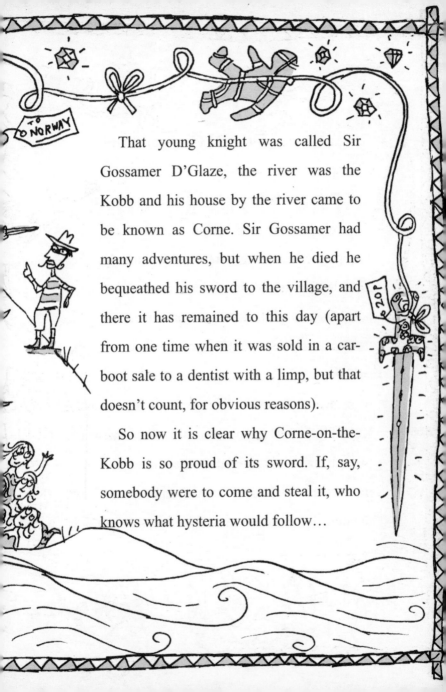

That young knight was called Sir Gossamer D'Glaze, the river was the Kobb and his house by the river came to be known as Corne. Sir Gossamer had many adventures, but when he died he bequeathed his sword to the village, and there it has remained to this day (apart from one time when it was sold in a car-boot sale to a dentist with a limp, but that doesn't count, for obvious reasons).

So now it is clear why Corne-on-the-Kobb is so proud of its sword. If, say, somebody were to come and steal it, who knows what hysteria would follow…

## Chapter 4

# The Hunt Begins

The long hot summer had toasted Corne-on-the-Kobb like a slice of granary bread on a beach holiday. The grass was parched and brown, the flow of the River Kobb had ebbed to a thirsty trickle and several pigeons had a serious case of sunburn. This was the worst drought that the Kobb Valley had seen since 1915, when the whole place became a savannah and some lions moved in and ate everybody. But that's another story and the lions have politely asked me not to mention it.

Casper and Lamp crunched through the sun-baked park towards the village square. Lamp was dawdling behind, staring into space and smiling vacantly.

"What are you doing?" said Casper.

"I'm going to call it Daisy."

"Call what Daisy?"

"My lie detector. It's a lovely name."

Casper sighed. "That might get confusing. Someone's already got that name."

"Who?"

"Daisy."

Lamp scratched his head. "Oh yeah."

"How about The Bluff Boiler?"

"That's nice too." He galumphed forward and giggled. "I'm in love."

As the boys approached the square, the first thing they saw was 'Blossom's Bloomers', a little terraced shop where 'Murray's Doorknob and Salami Emporium' used to stand. Now it was fronted with a dark green awning and walls covered in flowering clematis. Outside the entrance were displayed hundreds of little plant pots holding geraniums, tulips and pansies of every colour, in front of muscular sunflowers and luscious lilacs. There was a queue of villagers trailing out of the door and halfway round the square, and more leaving the shop already loaded with bouquets of roses or baskets of wild grasses. The square itself was adorned with beautiful flowering wreaths on every door, window boxes filled with delicate petunias and vases stuffed full on every porch, beside every bench and lining the

steps to the village hall. Finally, flapping at the top of the flagpole on the village-hall roof was not the normal tattered flag, but the most gigantic bouquet of multicoloured hydrangeas the world had ever seen since the world's biggest hydrangea bouquet competition last year, which, admittedly, had some pretty massive bouquets of hydrangeas.

"Wow," cooed Casper. "They must make a killing."

"I'm going to buy some flowers for Daisy," said Lamp.

"She's probably got enough already."

Through the window Casper could see Daisy wrapping up a large bunch of peonies while Lavender snipped some sweet peas from their stems and presented them to a blushing gentleman. Casper dragged Lamp away from the shop and into the square where Mayor Rattsbulge was trying to gather a crowd. So far he'd only managed to attract the attention of Clemmie Answorth (still clanging her bell), old Mrs Trimble and the flock of pigeons.

"Oi!" he shouted to the enormous flower shop queue, spraying greasy flecks of spit all over Mrs Trimble. "We've got an emergency here."

The queue members just grunted and shuffled forward a bit. More people joined the back, sighing longingly with flowery business cards clutched to their chests.

The mayor bellowed, "Come here, you scoundrels! This is no time for flowers."

"Ooh, are they selling flowers?" said Mrs Trimble, who owned twenty-six cats (all called Tiddles). She put on her spectacles and trotted

off to join the queue.

Mayor Rattsbulge had had enough. "Fine," he barked. "Nobody's getting the cash reward…"

At the words 'cash reward', the villagers' idiotic ears pricked up. They dropped whatever they were holding (such as babies, packed lunches or priceless Ming vases) and bounded towards the mayor like squirrels to a nut buffet, barging Casper and Lamp to the back of the crowd with well-placed elbows or teeth. Instantly the square was packed with penniless, greedy idiots, and the flower shop was empty.

"That's better," said Mayor Rattsbulge, taking a chomp of the Scotch egg that he'd put in his top pocket for emergencies.

"Oh, no, she's here," groaned Lamp, pointing to Casper's right where a skinny little girl with long brown hair and a hawk nose approached them, hand in hand with her pointy mother.

Casper winced. "Anemonie Blight."

In a recent poll, Anemonie Blight was voted the most evil girl in the cosmos (pushing the previous winner, Empress Vandraga 'Slayer of Children' into second place). Made from a pint of pure hate and a sprinkling of malice, then oven-baked in the furnaces of hell, Anemonie was only happy once she'd made somebody cry. Two weeks ago she'd burst Teresa Louncher's eardrum in a game of Rock, Paper, Nuclear Explosion. Last time Anemonie had seen Casper, she punched him so hard that even Lamp got a nosebleed.

"She's coming this way," quavered Lamp, visibly shaking.

Casper crossed his fingers and closed his eyes.

Anemonie was close – not more than five metres away now. He held his breath, prepared for the pain and waited, and waited, and… oddly, nothing happened. Casper dared to open an eye. Anemonie had walked straight past them, head down, hands deep in the pockets of her sickly pink jumpsuit.

Casper nudged Lamp, who had been cowering behind his hands. "She's gone," he said.

Lamp chewed his lip. "Why didn't she hit me?"

"I know. That's not like her at all."

Casper watched as Anemonie stopped next to her pointy mother at a spot right at the back of the square and observed the scene from afar.

"Now, now," drawled Mayor Rattsbulge, "give me your attention or I'll raise taxes."

The villagers hung on to the mayor's every word like nits on a hippie's beard.

"Somebody…" Mayor Rattsbulge's bottom lip quivered, so he hid it behind a mouthful of Scotch egg. "Somebody…" – Scotch egg now swallowed – "has assaulted Betty Woons and stolen the bejewelled sword of Sir Gossamer de Glaze."

Those who hadn't already heard the news shrieked. Those who had already heard the news nodded knowingly, saying, "Haven't you heard?" and, "Horrible news," and made shrugging gestures.

"Now Betty doesn't remember a thing because the thief hit her quite hard on the head…"

Betty Woons grinned at the crowd and then slapped the top of her head with her withered hand, tutting loudly.

"…and nobody else witnessed the crime at all. In fact, the only clue we have is this." He felt around in his Scotch egg pocket and plucked out a wiry black cat's whisker.

The crowd gasped.

"Yes, we worried this day would come, and I fear it has. He's here. This whisker is the calling card of none other than the French cat burglar *Le Chat*!"

As those terrible words of *Le Chat* spread through the crowd like a snotty cold, jaws dropped in horror, eyes sprang with tears and mothers clutched on to their children like wriggly teddy bears. They'd all heard about him, they'd all been warned about him, but not once did they think he'd actually strike in Corne-on-the-Kobb.

"Now, few people have seen him in the flesh, but we believe him to look something like this." Mayor Rattsbulge held aloft a large poster featuring a photograph of a regular black cat, with

the words WANTED – dead or alive (preferably dead) hastily scribbled along the top in big black letters, and *Artist's impression at the bottom.

Audrey Snugglepuss gasped. "I've seen him."

Mrs Trimble went very pale. "But that's… that's Tiddles."

The crowd screamed and pointed at Mrs Trimble. One person threw a shoe.

"Calm down," bellowed Mayor Rattsbulge. "Nobody's blaming Tiddles."

The crowd stopped screaming.

Mrs Trimble sobbed, reached into her bag and dried her eyes on a newborn kitten.

The mayor straightened his mayoral gown (which he'd made himself by stapling together three rolls of red carpet material) and continued. "Now, the roads out of the village were guarded last night, and they have been ever since. This has given me valuable time to think about how to catch this scoundrel, and you'll be pleased to know I've got a plan!"

Casper, who had been watching Anemonie Blight and her mother, noticed them become distinctly twitchier as the meeting progressed. Anemonie kept rubbing her wrists, and her mother couldn't stand still.

"It's a foolproof plan if I may say so myself, both

original and unpredictable. It's taken me nearly all day and three whole pies to think of it, but here it is…" He did a drum roll on Mitch McMassive's bald head. "You find *Le Chat* for me!"

"Hurray!" cheered the villagers, applauding their mayor's genius plan most wholeheartedly.

"Whoever can catch *Le Chat* and retrieve the sword will be rewarded with…" Mayor Rattsbulge pulled a wad of crumpled banknotes out of his pocket and hastily counted them. "One… two… two… five…" Losing count, he shrugged and shouted, "Twenty-thousand pounds."

The crowd went, "Oooooooh!"

"And…" The mayor rooted around in another pocket, producing something brown and sticky. "…The rest of this pie."

The crowd went, "Aaaaaah!"

Sandy Landscape rolled up his sleeves. "Cor, imagine that – twenty grand. I'm gonner gold-plate my wellies."

"I'm going to gold-plate my house," said Audrey Snugglepuss.

"I'm going to gold-plate my cats," said Mrs Trimble.

"'Ere, can I have half o' that money now if I promise to find the sword?" shouted Sandy.

"No chance." Audrey yanked him back by his belt loop. "It's mine."

"You'll have to get past me first," squeaked Mitch McMassive, launching himself at Audrey's legs and bundling her to the ground, knocking over Clemmie Answorth in the process. Sandy Landscape dived on top, launching punches into the crowd. Then, with a left hook, he felled old

Mrs Trimble, who shrieked and dropped her bag of cats. The cats tumbled out into the melee, ripping and nipping with furry fury.

"SILENCE!" bellowed Mayor Rattsbulge.

Cats and villagers alike froze and stared at their mayor. Sandy Landscape let go of Mitch McMassive's head and put his teeth back in.

"One more thing. There's a dangerous criminal on the loose, and I don't want any more of my villagers hurt than is necessary. So I'm imposing a curfew: everybody must stay in their houses after dark. Understood?"

"Yes, Mayor Rattsbulge," chorused the villagers.

"What about the Summer Ball?" came the shrill tones of Audrey Snugglepuss from somewhere beneath Sandy Landscape's foot. "That's tomorrow,

and the cake's all ready." The Corne-on-the-Kobb Carrot Cake Appreciation Society, of which Audrey was the president, baked a giant cake every year for the occasion. "Will all those carrots have died for nothing, mister mayor?"

Audrey's question got a roar of agreement from the villagers. The Summer Ball was a much-loved event in Corne-on-the-Kobb – you got free wine and sausage rolls all night, and the best-dressed villager won a pig.

"Of course the ball will still take place." Mayor Rattsbulge wouldn't dream of cancelling it, not while there were free sausage rolls and a massive cake, anyway. "But no loitering outside. We'll lock the doors once you're all in. Now clear off, and find my sword."

The crowd cheered as the mayor waddled down

from his perch, then they promptly got back to beating chunks out of each other with handbags, wooden legs, or whatever else was to hand.

"Come on, Lamp," said Casper, just as Mitch McMassive flew straight past them and crashed into a bin. "Let's go home before things get any uglier."

As they left the square, Casper could feel the gaze of the little pointy-nosed girl burn the back of his neck. "I don't trust Anemonie," he said. "Did you see how shifty she's acting?"

"Not as shifty as him." Lamp nodded towards an olive-skinned little man with a black beret, whom Casper swore he'd never noticed before. He sat on a low wooden stool by the steps to the village hall, his pursed white lips sucking on a needle-thin cigarette. He watched the mass brawl with a smirk.

"Who's that?"

"He looks weird."

"He looks French, Lamp."

"Like *Le Splat*."

"Yeah, like—" Casper gasped. "Do you think he's part of it?"

But Lamp wasn't listening. He was too busy waving through the window at Daisy. She grinned and waved back, giving Lamp a minor heart attack.

## Chapter 5

# Buns and Biscuits

Families are odd things. They come in all shapes and sizes, colours and smells. Some families grow on trees, some families come by post and some families arrive off the train with a bulging suitcase and a head full of dreams. The biggest family in the world contains two fathers, three mothers, twelve grandmothers, twenty-six brothers and a poodle. The smallest family in the world is so minute that it can only be seen through a special microscope. The Wriggle family of Essex makes a living by travelling the world and juggling ducks. There is

a rumour of a new sort of family that exists only on the Internet, which can be downloaded in bite-size chunks for a weekly fee. All of these are examples of the wonderful, remarkable or downright laughable sorts of families that you can get these days. But none of these even come close to the insanity of the Candlewacks family of Corne-on-the-Kobb.

"I'm home," called Casper as he slammed the sticky front door behind him.

"Casper, that you? Come on through, supper's looking delicious!" Casper's mum's shout from the kitchen was accompanied by the clattering of knives and a rubbery thud.

On the doormat lay five red letters all with different shouty words on the front like Urgent: Final Payment Request and Fines overdue – we will release the hounds, along with one of those Wanted posters with that picture of Tiddles on it. Casper picked them all up and traipsed down the dark corridor to the back of the house. At the kitchen table sat Casper's dad, Julius Candlewacks, surrounded by mountains of cookery books and furiously scribbling on a roll of toilet paper. Casper's mum, Amanda Candlewacks, stood proudly in the middle of the cluttered kitchen floor, her blouse inside out, little pink rollers littering her straggled blonde hair, with a whole raw chicken clutched to her chest like a slippery hot water bottle.

"I'm making chicken!" she announced.

"Oh," said Casper, worried. "It looks very dirty. What have you been doing with it?"

"I might have dropped it once or twice, but it's fine. We always clean the floor, right?"

"I've never cleaned the floor."

"It doesn't matter, Casper. Floor bits are tasty." Amanda flung open the oven door, threw in the chicken, slammed it shut and grinned. "Simple as that. I'm a natural!"

The door swung back open and broke right off its hinges, tipping the oven forward so that the grubby chicken tumbled out on to the floor and rolled under a cupboard.

"Oh…" muttered Amanda. "Is that meant to happen?"

Casper sighed. "Forget the chicken, Mum.

Let's try beans on toast."

"Beans on toast! That's easy." She perked up at once and bounded back over to the stove, grabbing the nearest saucepan and thumping it down on a ring. Into the pan she threw two slices of stale bread and a tin of baked beans (unopened), then she stepped back with hands on hips, chest puffed up proudly. "There. I'm not completely useless."

"Um…"

You see, being a mum is a difficult job. It's much easier, on balance, to sit in front of the telly and munch biscuits. Amanda Candlewacks made this discovery eleven and a half years ago, shortly after the birth of her bubbly blonde-haired son called Casper. She'd only get up from the sofa during advert breaks or weather reports, and that would only be to fetch biscuits, use the toilet or have another baby (which only happened once, and Amanda was furious about it because she missed the latest episode of *Granny's Skin Complaints*).

But two months ago the telly broke and, left alone in the house with Cuddles, her screaming baby, Amanda was faced with a problem. You see, televisions have 'mute' buttons and you can change the channel when you get bored, but even the most up-to-date babies can't boast those features. So she was forced to be a mother for the very first time in eleven and a half years. Strangely, she quite liked it. Not so strangely (for someone who'd been sitting in front of a telly for over a decade), she wasn't very good at it.

"Dad, can't you help?" pleaded Casper. "You're a chef, for goodness' sake."

Julius didn't look up from his toilet paper. "*Was*

a chef, Casp. *Was*."

"Whatever. Couldn't you cook our dinner?"

"I'm busy, can't you see?"

Casper sighed. Two months ago Julius Candlewacks's restaurant had closed down due to bad press and a small explosion, and suddenly he'd found himself without a job. Never one to give up, he jumped on the next bus to High Kobb, took out every single book from the food section of Kobb Central Library, staggered home and announced to his family, "I'm writing a celebrity cookbook!"

"Which celebrity?" Casper had asked.

"Me, of course. I've been a chef for twenty years; now it's time to pass on my knowledge."

"What knowledge?" Casper had asked.

But Julius wouldn't hear a word of it. From that moment on he spent every waking second poring over exotic ingredient lists, copying down useful pages and growing steadily more angry about younger chefs' successes.

Today was no different. "Look at this potato gratin, Casp, just look at it." He waggled a loose page from *Vinnie's Veg* across the room. "It isn't even properly seasoned! That's it. I'm taking this one. He doesn't deserve it."

"Dad, you can't just steal other people's recipes."

"I'm not! Mine'll have more seasoning."

Casper rubbed his eyes. "Never mind. Where's Cuddles?" Normally he would've heard screaming by now, or at least felt that characteristic stabbing pain as his feral baby sister bit him on the ankle.

"She's hanging on the line," said Amanda. "I gave her a wash today."

"Hanging on the…?"

"I couldn't very well put her in the tumble dryer, could I?" Amanda burst into trills of uproarious laughter.

Eleven and a half straight years of telly would do funny things to anyone, but Casper hoped his mother might have learnt how to be a bit less bonkers by now. This morning he'd caught Amanda drying her hair with a Hoover. Last night she'd plugged a dummy up each of Cuddles' nostrils. "These things take time," he told himself.

Casper shoved open the back door and dashed into the garden, where the ten-month-old bundle of teeth and snot called Cuddles Candlewacks

bounced up and down inside a pair of Julius's boxer shorts that were hanging on the washing line. At the sight of Casper she screeched like a wounded eagle and swung her arms about, gnashing at the air with her tiny razor-sharp fangs.

"Come on, let's get you inside." Casper unhooked Cuddles and carried her at arm's length back to the kitchen.

"There she is!" Amanda grabbed the baby from Casper's arms and gave her a loving squeeze. "Ooh, 'WANTED'. What's this about?" She reached for the poster.

Instantly forgotten, Cuddles slithered gently down her mother's legs. She landed on all fours and scuttled off under the cupboard to hunt the raw chicken.

"Haven't you heard?" said Casper. "Someone's stolen Sir Gossamer D'Glaze's sword. A jewel thief going by the name of *Le Chat*."

"Is this him?" asked Amanda. "Poor feller. He does look so much like a cat."

Cuddles' head popped out from under the cupboard. She stared at Amanda with wild eyes.

"What's she doing?" Casper frowned at his sister, her ears pricked up attentively.

"Oh, it's her new thing. She saw a cat in the garden and went berserk. Started bonking her head against the windows."

"TAT!" screeched Cuddles. "TAT!"

"Ooh!" Amanda frowned. "She's not done that before."

"She's saying 'cat'!" Casper couldn't believe his ears.

"Don't be silly," giggled Amanda. "Babies can't talk."

"TATATA! TATATA!"

"No, she is, she definitely is!"

Cuddles scrabbled out from under the cupboard and set off on a circuit of the kitchen, her nose frantically sniffing the air.

"Is it the cat?" Casper waved the poster at Cuddles. "Do you want the cat?"

Cuddles' whole body tensed. Then she launched at Casper, scaling his trousers, yapping with all her lungs, drool dangling off her sticky chin. She leapt vertically, snatching the poster from Casper's hands and then dropping to the floor.

Casper had never seen Cuddles chase a cat, but he was pretty sure he knew what would happen next. "Cuddles, don't—"

But he was wrong. Cuddles wasn't tearing it to pieces. She wasn't even gnawing at the cat's face. Actually, she'd wrapped both of her arms round the poster and was rolling around with it on the floor, gurgling strings of happy nonsense and licking its ear.

"TATATA!" Cuddles squealed, before returning to her cat cuddle.

Casper grinned. "She knew the word, Mum. She said 'Cat'!"

"Her first word!" Amanda skipped over to Cuddles and swung her around in the air (covering herself in sticky splats of toddler slobber as she spun). "Julius, darling, our baby's said her first word!"

"Shh," Julius retorted. "I'm working."

Amanda swung Cuddles even faster round her head. "Casper, get the camera."

"We don't have a camera."

"Oh, she's a genius! She's a genius, Casper. Bring her the dictionary."

"We don't have a dictionary."

"My beautiful little Cuddles!" Mother and wailing baby spun round and round, quicker and quicker. But the spinning got too fast, Cuddles coughed up a chicken bone and with a shriek she slipped from her mother's hands. Time slowed as Casper watched his sister soar through the air, leaving a slimy dribble vapour trail in her wake. She lost altitude, dropped like a stone and landed with a *Schmulck* face-first in the mouldy fruit bowl.

Amanda and Casper held their breath.

There was a gurgle, then a squeak, then Cuddles climbed out of the bowl grinning from ear to ear and covered in rotten banana.

"She's alive!" Amanda raced over to greet her aeronautic baby. "Aren't I a clever little mummy, putting that fruit bowl just where you'd land?"

"Come on, give her here," said Casper. "Your beans smell burnt."

"Ooh, forgot about them!"

Casper plonked Cuddles down on top of a pile of cookbooks on the kitchen table, found the least sticky seat and sat down next to Julius.

"Good, Casp, I need your help. I was going to call my book *The Candlewacks Cookbook*. Now I know what you're thinking – snore, snore. Well, *exactly.* But then I had a brainwave. Call it a stroke of genius. I'm calling the book… wait for it… *Juicy Julius.*" He spelt out the words in the air with a grand flash of his wrists.

There was a long pause. Casper chewed his tongue.

"What d'you think?"

Luckily there was no need to answer because a heavy saucepan thumped down on to the table in front of them, held by the grinning Amanda. "Dinner is served," she announced proudly.

Black plumes of smoke poured from the pan (due to the burnt toast and the half-melted tin of beans), stinging Casper's eyes worse than Lamp's nettle sunglasses. Covering his mouth with his T-shirt, Casper blundered blindly across

the kitchen and threw open the door. "Let's have supper in the garden."

"Great idea!" Amanda sang, "I do so love picnics." She disappeared down the garden with the saucepan in a puff of smoke (literally).

"Right. Time for some proper dinner." Casper searched the kitchen cupboards, but all he found worth eating was a pile of rice (with the weevils picked out), a carton of orange juice and half a sausage. "*Sausage a l'Orange*," he said determinedly and reached for the kettle. "Dad, why don't you ever cook any more?"

"Too busy. We're on to chapter five, Casper. 'Buns and Biscuits'. What are my good ones?"

"Don't know," Casper replied. "Not those squashed fly biscuits you used to do, though."

"But they were great!"

"They had actual flies, Dad. It's meant to be raisins."

"I knew that." Julius coughed and a large book mountain came tumbling down. "You're no help at all, Casper."

"I just think your book idea is silly, that's all. You do realise there's no money in publishing?"

"Course there is. Everyone'll want a copy of my book. I'm a household name."

Casper chuckled. "Which household?"

"This one."

"Any others?"

"I'm working on that." Julius puffed up his chest. "Anyway, don't just stand around being useless. We're looking for buns and biscuits." He picked up the nearest book and flung it at Casper, who dropped his wooden spoon just in time to catch the book.

He read the title – *Just My Tripe: 1000 tasty uses for cow's stomach*. "Yuck. You sure I'll find any biscuits in here?"

"Or buns, Casper. The chapter's called 'Biscuits and Buns', remember?"

"How could I forget?" Casper groaned and flicked through *Just My Tripe*'s greasy pages. *Tripe 'n' Kidney Soup; Ripe Tripe Roulade; Edible Tripe Shoes with Rhubarb Laces...*"

"Pah!" Julius pointed at a recipe on the top of his pile. "Found a mistake, Casper. *Juicy Julius* won't have any mistakes."

"What's that then?" asked Casper. He soon wished he hadn't.

Julius pointed at the page. "These biscuits are called *Langues de Chat.*"

Cuddles suddenly turned to face Julius, eyes wide.

"Now I know a bit of French from my gap year, but I've looked through the recipe and I don't see a single cat tongue."

"TATATA?" squeaked Cuddles frantically.

Casper dashed over to calm his sister down. "Shh, don't listen to Daddy." He pressed his finger to his mouth and glared at Julius.

"I'm serious! *Langues de Chat* means 'Cat Tongues'. That's just a lie! I don't see even a slice of cat."

"TAT!" squealed Cuddles. "TATATA!"

She sprang into action and set upon Julius's books, clawing and tearing through the flimsy pages trying to find the cat.

"No!" Julius yelled, sweeping Cuddles from his

mauled books. "Get off. That's my hard work! You can't!"

She could. Cuddles jumped back on and ripped more furiously, flinging empty dust covers over her shoulders once she'd checked each one for cats. Casper dived for cover inside the oven and watched the rest of the action from there.

After two minutes Cuddles' claws hit hard wood and she sat back, puzzled. She sniffed once, twice, then flumped over the side of the table and scuttled on all fours down the corridor.

Julius looked with horror at the scene.

"Dad, I'm sorry," said Casper, still in the oven.

His dad watched the pile of torn paper for what seemed like ages. Then suddenly, his eyes lit up. "Don't touch anything, Casper. Where's the glue?"

"I don't think that's going to—"

"Rubbish. I'll stick it all back together." He tiptoed to the cutlery drawer and rummaged around before pulling out an old glue stick. "Don't breathe. Don't even think of breathing. Don't even think of thinking of breathing." Gingerly, he picked up the nearest two shreds. "No..." he said, and placed them back down. He picked up two more. "Ah!" he whispered, unscrewing the top of the glue. "This isn't so hard. I've always been good at puzzles."

"Delish!" sang Amanda as she re-entered the kitchen and threw the blackened pan into the sink.

A gust of wind followed her through the door, lifting a million scraps of paper high into the air. Half of them swirled out of the door and flew off into the sky; the other half-million wafted solemnly to the sticky kitchen floor and... well... stuck.

When Casper looked back at Julius, his face was in his hands.

"It's OK, Dad. You can start again."

"Twenty-thousand pounds, Casp," he said, a little teary.

"What's that?"

"Course I don't really want to write a book. I'm a chef. Cooking is my life. Olive oil runs in my veins; my heart beats a spicy rhythm with a chicken drumstick on the bongos of my soul."

Casper frowned. "And twenty thousand pounds…?"

"I want my restaurant back, I really do. But I can't open another one, not without lots of equipment. Lots of equipment costs lots of money, Casp, and lots of money costs twenty-thousand pounds. All I've got is…" Julius turned out the pockets of his stained chef's trousers, finding twelve pence and a lollipop. He wiggled the lollipop in front of Casper's eyes. "I'll sell you this for twenty grand?"

All of a sudden a bell rang in the back of Casper's mind as he recalled Mayor Rattsbulge's speech. "How much did you say you needed?"

"Twenty thousand. It's strawberry flavour."

"Forget the lollipop, Dad." His head was buzzing now. "I've got a better plan."

Julius shrugged and popped it in his mouth.

## Chapter 6

# First Encounter

"…And now it's time for 'How to Catch a Criminal', with your host, Detective Cuffbert 'Cuffs' Parkhurst."

"Now this is more like it." Casper sat forward on the sofa, his pencil and notepad held at the ready. The mayor had been perfectly clear: whoever brought home *Le Chat* and the sword would earn twenty thousand pounds; just what Julius needed to get his restaurant started.

The television cut to a butch policeman with a crew cut and a nose ring, squeezing the breath out of two roughed-up youths, one under each arm. "'Allo. I'm Detective Cuffbert Parkhurst, but you better call me 'Cuffs' unless you want a fick ear. I've nicked over a million criminals in my life. In fact these two oiks are my million-and-twelf and million-and-firteenf." He banged the youths' heads together and bundled them into a patrol car. "So if you break the law, you'll 'ave Cuffs at your door…"

Casper didn't know a thing about fighting crime, so he'd set himself in front of Cops 'n' Robbers TV, one of those rubbish cable channels that you'd never watch unless Cuddles had eaten the remote again. For two hours he'd been watching grainy car-chase footage broken up by insurance adverts, but this show seemed more promising. Casper licked his pencil.

"Now, the first fing you gotta remember if you wanna be like me," Cuffs prodded a tattooed thumb at himself and snarled, "is that the criminal always returns to the scene of the crime. The night after 'e's done it, once it's dark, 'e'll go back to check nuffin's outta place. Get that into yer heads and you know where to start lookin'."

"Of course!" Casper sat bolt upright, a sudden flash of inspiration hitting him right between the temples. "Perfect! Thanks, Cuffs. Wait there." Casper dashed out of the living room and up the stairs, narrowly missing Cuddles, who was gnawing on the carpet. By the time Casper reached his bedroom the plan was fully formed in his head.

Some say that a boy's room perfectly reflects his mind. Casper's room was an intriguing mess. Clothes and books were strewn across the floor and piled up in corners, crushing model planes, plastic tanks and sheets of scrap paper scrawled with mythical beasts. On the far side was an ant farm, front pane smashed by a cricket ball and ants tumbling out through the cracks, down on to the grubby carpet below and off under the wardrobe. Back down the same path returned another line of victorious ants proudly carrying chunks of chocolate biscuit. A pair of muddy shoes stood on his bed next to a science experiment, which, by the looks of the blue foam drizzling on to the carpet, had been a failure.

With a couple of nimble leaps over three weeks of dirty laundry, Casper reached the other side of his room and rooted around among the mess. He fished out a tin can attached to a string leading out of his window.

"Lamp," he whispered into the can. "Are you there?" Casper could make out snoring on the other end. "Lamp!" he rasped, as loudly as he dared.

There was a grunt and a heavy bump. "Daisy?" mumbled Lamp.

"No, it's Casper."

"Oh. Can you put Daisy on?"

"She's not here, Lamp. Were you asleep?"

"Yes. Very."

"Sorry, Lamp. But this is an emergency."

"Can't we do it in the morning?"

"No, that's too late. We have to go now."

"Go where?"

"I'll be outside your house in ten minutes. Tell you then."

"What about the fur queue?"

"The fur queue?"

"No, I mean the perfume."

"What perfume?"

"The Corfu. The curlew, the… Oh, I don't know what it is, Casper. The rule where we're not allowed outside at night."

Casper held back a giggle. "You mean the curfew?"

"That's what I said." Lamp sounded frustrated.

"We'll just have to be extra quiet. Bring your sponge shoes."

"Yesss."

Hearing a clunk and some shuffling on the other end, Casper got on with preparations. He grabbed a holey black jumper and pulled on a woolly blue hat to cover his hair. Into his backpack he threw his torch (for light), a penknife (for protection) and an apple (in case he wanted an apple). Then he found his stiff leather belt and a handful of dog biscuits (left over from a failed attempt to house-train Cuddles) and he was ready. With the bag lugged over his shoulder, Casper padded out of his room as silently as his shoes would allow. It only took one wave of a miniature crunchy bone biscuit to grab Cuddles' attention. She pricked up her nose, sniffed and bounded through the hall towards Casper, leaping upwards, jaws first, at his hand. With one swift move Casper snatched the biscuit away, grabbed the scruff of Cuddles' neck and looped one end of the leather belt round her frilly collar. With Cuddles safely restrained, he popped the bone biscuit in her mouth to keep her quiet and shoved her under his arm. Then he headed out through the front door, closing it softly behind him.

Night-time in Corne-on-the-Kobb is basically the same as daytime, except all the idiots are replaced by darkness and the shops are closed. Sometimes one of the villagers forgets to go to bed and just saunters around town wondering who turned off the lights, but not tonight, not with the curfew.

The deserted streets still held the day's warmth, which had softened the tarmac under Casper's feet to a tacky mess, a similar texture to the crust on his dad's famous cough-syrup sponge. Cuddles scuttled along in front, straining on the leather belt and occasionally stopping to sniff a tree trunk

or gobble some crumbs. At the end of Cracklin'
Crescent Casper turned right, and then right again
towards Lamp's garage.

Lamp appeared from beneath the shadows in
a pair of pale-blue stripy pyjamas and matching
nightcap, plus his home-made pair of sponge shoes

(useful for super-silent tiptoeing and mopping up spillages). He blinked in the moonlight and rubbed his eyes. "I hope this is important, Casper," Lamp grumbled. "I was dreaming about dolphins."

"Sorry Lamp, but this is huge."

Lamp looked at Casper and frowned. "It looks normal size."

"I learnt three new things tonight," Casper continued. "First, Cuddles absolutely loves ca—"

"TAT?"

"Never mind that one. She might come in useful, that's all, because second, we *need* to catch..." – he dropped his voice to a whisper – "*Le Chat*."

"Yes, we do," whispered Lamp, nodding knowingly. "Do we? Why?"

"For the reward money."

"I don't need money, though." Lamp got everything he needed from the Kobb-Valley rubbish tip, where you can have all the scrap metal you want if you say hello to Mr Flee and pat his dogs.

"No, for my dad," said Casper. "He needs his restaurant back, and he can't do it without twenty thousand pounds."

"Can't he just go and ask Mr Flee and pat his dogs?"

"Mr Flee doesn't give away restaurants, Lamp. That's something you have to buy."

"Oh." Lamp nodded and made a mental note to write that down.

"Anyway, the third thing I learnt is that the criminal always returns to the scene of the crime."

"Why would they do that?"

"'To check nuffin's outta place'," Casper said, doing his best impression of Cuffs Parkhurst. It hurt his throat, so he went back to normal. "Rub out any fingerprints – that sort of thing."

Lamp looked at his fingers for a bit and then shrugged. "Which one's the prince?"

"Prints, Lamp. Whenever you touch something your fingers leave marks."

"That's clever." Lamp pulled an impressed face and tried to shake his own hand.

"My point is this – we know where we can find *Le*—" Casper remembered Cuddles and stopped himself.

"Splat," helped Lamp.

"TAT!"

Casper stuffed a dog biscuit into Cuddles's mouth. "Yes, and with Cuddles we've got the

99

perfect catcher. She's started chasing… erm…"
– he spelt it out – "C, A, Ts, you see, but not to
catch them. She loves them."

Lamp couldn't spell so he had no idea what
Casper was on about.

Casper continued. "So we let her at *Le*… the cat
burglar, she'll cuddle him to the ground and we get
the twenty thousand pounds!"

Lamp wrinkled his face. "Do we have to? I'm
tired and the dolphins are waiting."

"I thought you liked saving the day," said
Casper, disappointed.

"But it's not the day," said Lamp, pointing at
the moon. "It's the night, and that's when you're
s'posed to be in bed." He looked up at his window
longingly.

"Come on, Lamp, please? For my dad?"

Casper didn't want to admit it, but adventures weren't the same without Lamp.

Silence fell while Lamp thought about it, punctuated only by the sound of Cuddles gnawing on Casper's shoe. Eventually Lamp sighed. "All right, I'll come. I can dream about dolphins in the morning."

"Great," grinned Casper. "Let's go."

"Where?"

"The village vault." Casper yanked Cuddles out of a rabbit hole and set off towards the village square, with Lamp shuffling behind, muttering to himself something about portable duvets. They passed through the moonlit park where a cool breeze disturbed the parched earth and blew little clouds of dust around, stinging Casper's eyes.

"Casper?" said Lamp.

"Hm?"

"Who do you think it is then? I mean *Le*—"

"Yeah, I know who you mean. Wouldn't put it past Anemonie." Casper scowled at the thought of her. "She's done far worse."

"What about that smoking man we saw in the square?"

"The French-looking one? Could be him."

"Or Napoleon."

"But he's not alive, Lamp."

"I see your point," said Lamp, sucking his finger. "He is French, though. What about Dracula? He's always doing naughty things. Or Darth Vader."

Casper sighed.

The three reached the end of the park and stepped on to the cobbled street leading to the village square.

"Stop," hissed Casper, spotting the light from a torch up ahead. "Someone's on patrol."

Lamp huffed. "How can we get to the vault now?"

"No idea. Shh! We'll get a bit closer." Casper popped another doggy treat into Cuddles' mouth to keep her quiet, and together they crept through the shadowed street towards the square.

"Get down!" They dived behind a big plant pot in front of Blossom's Bloomers just in time to avoid the swish of the sentry's torch. Casper gripped Cuddles' lips tight and mouthed at Lamp, "Don't. Make. A. Noise." The torch swept past again, followed by the sound of slow footsteps.

Cuddles gurgled.

The torch swung towards them. "'Ere, oo's there?" It was the voice of village gardener Sandy

Landscape, not five metres away, and getting closer. "Come out and show yerself."

Cowering behind his conifer, Casper didn't even dare to breathe. Trembling, he shut his eyes tight and crossed his terrified fingers.

Suddenly, from across the square came another sound. It was a girl's voice, muffled and indistinct. "Oy, Sandy, over here."

"Eh?" Sandy grunted. He spun round and galloped out of the square in pursuit of the voice.

Lamp exhaled and sagged his head. "I thought we were goners."

"I recognise that voice," said Casper. "I'm sure of it."

"Now that you mention the Bluff Boiler," said Lamp (who obviously hadn't been listening), "I think I've got it working. All it needed was the spinny bit from an electric whisk and half a packet of cornflakes to get the motor running."

"Shh! Tell me about it later." Casper only turned round for an instant, but when he turned back two things had changed. Firstly the door to the village vault was hanging open just a crack, and secondly, a soft light glowed from inside.

"We've missed him! He's in there already."

"He didn't even knock," said Lamp.

"Jewel thieves never knock. They don't have to."

"Well, that's just rude."

"Come on, let's get a closer look."

The square was deserted now. Sandy Landscape was far away, chasing through dark streets yelling rude words at shadows. Casper, Lamp and Cuddles darted towards the vault. A glance through the front window sent Casper's heart thumping. He ducked down, grabbing Cuddles and cowering behind the safety of the wall. *Le Chat was right there!* He dared to peep through the window again. Dressed in a black leotard with a long thin tail, pricky-up ears and black whiskers, *Le Chat* slunk round the vault room wiping surfaces with a tiny black cloth. The light from inside cast skewed feline silhouettes of the mystery cat burglar on to the inside of the open door.

Cuddles spotted the shadow. Her face suddenly tensed.

"TATATATA!" screeched Cuddles, tugging wildly on the leather belt and straining with fury against Casper's grip. The silhouette sat bolt upright.

"Now, Cuddles!" yelled Casper, unleashing the beast with a flick of his wrist. "Go get him!"

From inside the vault came a woman's scream and the gnash of teeth followed by more yelps, the tinkling of glass, and then silence.

Casper sprang to his feet and rushed into the vault with Lamp hot on his tail. Inside was chaos: broken glass and toppled chairs lined the floor, but no *Le Chat* and *no Cuddles*.

"Where've they gone?"

"Through here," called Lamp, pointing to a smashed window at the back of the room. On one of the sharp edges dangled a shred of pink ribbon flapping happily in the late-evening breeze.

"Cuddles?" Casper wrenched the window open and clambered out, falling to the glass-sprinkled ground with a crunch. Lamp belly-flopped from the windowsill and landed on top of him, knocking the wind from his lungs.

"Where are they?" wheezed Casper. "Where are they?" But there was no sign of *Le Chat* or Cuddles, just an empty road scattered with broken glass and a lonely fox watching the action from an alleyway.

As a bewildered Sandy Landscape returned to find the vault door wide open for the second night running, Casper and Lamp stumbled through deserted back streets, picking shards of splintered glass out of areas they didn't even know they had.

## Chapter 7

# Dawn of the Detectives

The first cracks of sunlight peeped over the horizon. Morning flooded the streets of Corne-on-the-Kobb, chasing night (which is a total wimp and terrified of sunlight) back to its underground lair. Casper and Lamp were still out, searching in bins and under loose bits of pavement. They'd found some bricks, half a cheese sandwich (which Lamp shared with a lonely fox) and Sandy Landscape napping in an alley, but they hadn't found Cuddles. There was no sign of the missing baby. She was

well and truly lost.

"We say nothing, OK?" said Casper, limping on his left leg.

Lamp dragged his feet on the tarmac.

"Did you hear me, Lamp?"

"I was practising."

"You don't have to be completely silent. Just don't tell anyone we left our beds tonight."

"We did, Casper. I remember it."

"No, Lamp, listen. We have to tell them that we stayed in bed; otherwise we'll be in big trouble. Understand?"

"Big trouble…" Lamp looked at his grazed hands and sniffed. "Mum says I'm not to lie, Casper."

"She's right, but this is a special occasion. All we need to do is find Cuddles and we'll be fine.

Until then, we can't tell anyone what happened."

"What do I say then?"

"Just say you were asleep."

"Dreaming of dolphins?"

"Yes, dreaming of dolphins."

"I s'pose I can do that." Lamp bit his lip and spent the rest of the walk home practising. "No, Mum, I was at home, asleep, dreaming of dolphins," he repeated. "I can't have been out of bed, officer. I was dreaming of dolphins, you see."

Casper patted his friend on the back and sighed. This wasn't going to be easy.

If Casper had expected to see Cuddles patiently panting by the front door chewing a long black tail and looking pleased with herself, he was dismayed to find nothing but his old pair of wellies and the lonely fox. Even if he dressed the fox in pink and sharpened its teeth, it still wouldn't look anything like Cuddles. Casper turned his key in the lock and tiptoed in, past his snoring father and the blaring telly, up the creaking stairs and into his room. It was only after collapsing on to his bed that the full force of Casper's actions struck home – he'd gone and lost the baby.

"How am I going to get out of this one?" he asked the ceiling.

The ceiling didn't respond.

Even though he'd been up all night, Casper, lying fully clothed on his bed, didn't close his eyes and he didn't fall asleep. Right now, somewhere out there, Cuddles was screaming and biting and banging her little head – but where? He hadn't a clue. And then *Le Chat*'s scream.

Was he… was *she* a woman?

Twice Casper heard a bang outside, twice he sat bolt upright and leapt to the window, but it was only the lonely fox playing hopscotch. He even thought about going back out to look, but if he got caught then people would start asking questions. And not nice questions like, "Would you like some ice cream?" No – awkward questions like, "Why are you out after the curfew?" and "Does your mum know you're here?"

Casper tossed and turned through hours of sweaty fretting, listening to the birds' choir practice, until exhaustion overpowered his worry and he drifted off into a cloudy and restless sleep.

Thirty-eight seconds later, somebody shouted, "Found you!"

Casper awoke with a jolt as the somebody

grabbed his toes. "ARGH!" He bonked his head on the wall in his confusion.

Amanda emerged from the foot of his bed. "Sorry, darling. Thought you were Cuddles. We're playing hide-and-seek, you see." She tiptoed across the room and threw open Casper's wardrobe. "GOTCHA! Oh…" A pile of crumpled clothes and a startled mouse flumped out on to the floor, but Cuddles didn't.

With a purple lump swelling on the back of Casper's head and the morning sunlight stinging his eyes, Casper's brain didn't have space to remember why he'd only had thirty-eight seconds of sleep. But then the terrors of last night came flooding back and the pit of Casper's stomach dropped. Amanda wouldn't find Cuddles no matter how hard she looked.

"She's a good hider, I'll give her that," chuckled Amanda, bustling out of Casper's room and on to the landing. "But she's not won yet. You just wait until I check in... HERE! Bother."

He wanted to tell her everything. He wanted to explain what he'd done, why he'd done it and what he planned to do next. But he didn't dare; he just climbed out of bed and searched for his jeans. It took a groggy minute for Casper to realise he was still wearing them, as well as last night's T-shirt and shoes. Feeling too tired, too guilty, too absolutely rotten, he rolled out of his room without changing.

"I see you down there!" Dirty smalls and sweaty shirts flew across the landing as Amanda dived into the washing basket. She emerged with a pair of pants hung round each ear and holding a large bundle of pink socks. "Nope, not her after all. Smells the same though."

There was a knock at the door.

"You get it," sang Amanda, "I'm playing!" She skipped away to the bathroom to search down the toilet.

Casper trudged down the stairs feeling really sick and guiltier than ever, and pulled open the front door.

One-hundred-and-one unblinking eyes on fifty unblinking faces watched Casper from his drive. Instinctively, he slammed the door and leant on it, pinching himself hard in case he was dreaming. After all, he'd only managed thirty-eight seconds of sleep last night; it was entirely possible he'd fallen asleep halfway down the stairs. No such luck – the pinch just hurt.

There was another knock at the door.

Casper peeped through his letterbox at the waiting crowd. On the doorstep stood, well, everyone. There were short fat women, tall thin men and some somewhere in between. Some wore hats, some held cats, one man balanced on a unicycle. They couldn't have been from Corne-on-the-Kobb because Casper didn't recognise one face. "Who are you?"

An army of names invaded Casper's ears as the crowd all introduced themselves at the same time. The chap with the loudest voice was called Terry.

"And… um… what do you want?"

Casper's doorstep descended into a cacophony as each stranger described the purpose of his or her visit using poetry, puppets or interpretive dance. Someone near the front had brought a flipchart.

"Please stop."

The crowd fell silent.

"CAN WE COME IN, THEN?" shouted Terry.

"No. Listen, can one of you just tell me why you're here?"

"We're amateur detectives." A rubber-faced lady with red hair and an extra eye stepped forward and poked a voice recorder towards the letterbox. "We're investigating," she said.

The pit of Casper's stomach dropped. "Investigating what?"

"The robbery," shouted Terry.

"Why are you looking here, then?" Casper held his voice as steady as he could.

The crowd shrugged and looked at one another.

"I don't know," said an old man in shorts, "I just followed him." He pointed at Terry.

"ME?" Terry looked shocked. "BUT I WAS FOLLOWING HER."

All eyes turned to a tiny woman at the back. "C-c-crumbs," she stammered. "I'm just doing my shopping." She uttered a nervous titter and waddled away down the road.

Some of the crowd followed her, but most stayed behind.

"So…" Casper frowned through the letterbox.

"CAN WE COME IN NOW?" whispered Terry.

"No." Casper let the letterbox flap down.

There was yet another knock at the door.

"I'm not in," called Casper.

"OH," shouted Terry. "SORRY. WE'LL TRY SOMEWHERE ELSE."

The crowd seemed to disperse, so Casper made his way to the kitchen for some breakfast. With

all those detectives around it was going to be way harder to look for Cuddles without raising any suspicion, but there was no choice, he had to try.

"Hello, sonny Jim."

Casper yelped.

"Take a seat."

He did as he was told. The men in his kitchen didn't look like they knew what a joke was, let alone how to make one.

A gaunt, sunken-eyed gentleman sat on the opposite chair, horribly overdressed for the weather in a sharp black tail suit, navy-blue cravat, brown overcoat and matching deerstalker hat, all topped off with a mahogany pipe resting in the corner of his mouth. The stouter man standing behind him was equally suited, but he sported a bristling moustache, quizzical eyebrows, a bowler hat and a black bow tie.

"I could call my dad." Casper's hands shook.

"Better not," snarled the stouter man. He stomped round the table and blocked the doorway with his bulky frame.

Casper swallowed. "How did you get in here?"

"Wasn't hard," said the stouter man, pulling a crowbar from his back pocket and pointing it at an empty frame where the kitchen window used to be.

"Why do people keep breaking windows?" Casper asked. "Look, I don't know who you are, but you'd better leave."

"Oh, how rude of me." The gaunter man chuckled silently. "I didn't introduce myself. Headlock Bones, at your service." He proffered a gloved white hand across the table, but Casper didn't shake it. "And this is Wartson."

The man called Wartson grunted and put away his crowbar.

"We're doing a bit of investigation." Headlock Bones curled his upper lip and leant backwards on his chair, resting his leather boots on the table.

"I don't know anything." Casper's tongue had gone dry.

"Oh, but you do." Headlock Bones sat forward again, leaning right over the table until Casper could smell his minty breath. "Where's your sister?"

Casper stood up with a jerk, sending his chair clattering over behind him.

"Sit down, for goodness' sake. I just want a little chat."

He stood still, heart pounding in his chest.

"What do you know?"

"I ask the questions, sonny Jim, and anger'll get you nowhere. Now sit down."

Wartson picked up Casper's chair and shoved him back on to it with a rough palm.

"Isn't that better?" said Headlock Bones. "We don't want to hurt you, we just want our twenty thousand – understand?"

Casper nodded.

"We're not like those fools outside. We know how to get things done."

Wartson cracked his knuckles.

"And all we want to know is this… Where's your sister?"

Casper's eyes flicked from the men in his kitchen to the empty window leading to his back garden. An escape route, but could he do it? There was no choice. He took a deep breath, grinned at his pipe-smoking assailant and then leapt from his chair and vaulted through the empty window, out into the scorching summer morning.

"Get him!" roared Headlock Bones. But Casper was already round the corner, sprinting towards the garden gate. He flung it open and careered past the bewildered detectives milling about near his porch and away down the road. Twice he checked over his shoulder for pursuers, but nobody had followed him.

How had they known about Cuddles? Was it possible that they'd seen what happened last night? Casper forced the worry to the back of his mind and strode off towards Lamp's garage.

## Chapter 8

# Babynapped!

Lamp sat cross-legged on the ground surrounded by nuts, bolts and his Bluff Boiler, yapping away eagerly to a bearded detective with a notebook and an ear trumpet fastened on to the side of his head with a fat leather buckle.

"Don't tell him anything!" Casper sprinted over, almost colliding with Mavis and Bessie who had been politely preening themselves on the lawn. They clucked off inside, shaking their beaks and wondering what the world had come to when a pair of hens couldn't preen in peace any more.

"And where were you last night?" The detective

craned his ear trumpet towards Lamp.

Lamp stuck his face into the trumpet and shouted, "I was in bed," before turning to grin at Casper.

The detective licked his red crayon and scrawled the word 'Bread' in his notebook.

"Dreaming of dolphins," Lamp added.

"I see." He nodded, turned the page and wrote 'Golfing'. "And what about you?" The detective pointed his beard at Casper. "Anything to confess?"

"Nope, nothing."

"Aha." He added 'Muffin' to his notes. "Well, that's all I needed to know." He got up, tucked the crayon behind his ear trumpet and trotted off down the street.

"Oh, thank goodness for that," said Casper, clutching his chest.

"I lied, like you said." Lamp picked up the egg from the Bluff Boiler using an old rag and lopped the top off with a chisel. "Got a spoon?"

Casper's mouth fell open. "Lamp," he said, stunned, "your egg's boiled."

Lamp dunked his oily finger in the yolk and slurped it off. "Ow… hot! Tasty though."

"It works brilliantly! It picked up all those lies we told."

"Good for breakfast, anyway."

"Lamp, it's perfect."

"Is it?"

"Yes."

"Oh." Blushing, Lamp grinned and took another fingerful of egg. "Ow! Actually I prefer them hard-boiled. Where's my spanner?"

"Come on, we've got work to do." Casper

chuckled. "And bring that with you. We might need it."

The sun beat down on Corne-on-the-Kobb. In the park, more detectives pranced around, overturning bins and investigating their own feet through magnifying glasses. The deaf detective sat on a bench, scratching his ear trumpet, musing on the nonsense he'd scrawled in the notebook. Meanwhile five or six opportunistic others stood behind him copying his notes. But when they saw Casper and Lamp they galloped over, squawking, "Who's the murderer?" or "Where did you bury the necklace?" or "Is there a nice place nearby where we can get some lunch?" The boys put their heads down and raced towards the village square, batting off their advances like a fly swatter to dozens of oddly shaped flies. But if Casper had expected to find a similar scene in the centre of town, he was very, very disappointed. It was far worse. No less than two hundred amateur sleuths of every colour and shape imaginable (yes, even a purple octagon) had squeezed themselves into the square and swarmed about dementedly, accusing a collection of surrounded and bewildered villagers of embezzlement, gross negligence or high treason. Some were interviewing the pigeons; others were digging up the flowerbeds; one poor soul had somehow handcuffed himself to the minute hand of the town clock and was dangling fifteen metres above the ground, wailing soppily. Then the clock struck half past and he slid free, dropping into the crowd like a forgetful skydiver.

Lamp gulped. "Look, Casper. It's Lemony," he said, nodding his head to a shady corner nearby.

There slouched Anemonie Blight, staring right back at the boys with a sour sneer on her pointy face.

Normally Casper would be terrified of Anemonie. But then again, normally Anemonie would have him in a half nelson by now. Something was different about her, and Casper suddenly realised that the change in her behaviour had all started after *Le Chat* struck the village.

"Lamp, stick an egg on the Bluff Boiler," he whispered.

Lamp drew a large brown egg from his boiler-suit pocket and dusted it off, then placed it on the central dish.

"Hey, Anemonie."

"What." She pursed her lips and frowned, cowering further into the shadow.

"Where are you keeping Cuddles?"

"Dunno what you're talking about. Buzz off."

A podgy lady detective in sunglasses set up an easel and started sketching the three of them.

"Where's the sword?" Casper demanded.

Lamp nudged him with an elbow. "What's that on her arms?"

He was right, there were red scratches all over her skin.

"Nothing," she snapped, pulling her pink cardigan all the way to her wrists. "Leave me alone or I'll kick you."

"Casper, Lamp…" It was Daisy, wearing a dark green Blossom's Bloomers apron, trotting towards them and smiling radiantly.

Lamp went a bit melty, so Casper propped him up with a steady arm. "Hi, Daisy." She smelt of summer and happiness.

"I saw you go past. You all right?" Daisy asked.

"Fine, thanks." He wasn't fine – he was frightened and exhausted, and some butterflies had set up a holiday camp in his belly.

Daisy waved at Anemonie. "Cheer up."

Anemonie snorted.

Casper looked between the girls. "You know each other?"

"I was warned about her, that's all." Daisy turned back towards Casper and spotted the worry in his expression. "Oh, don't worry about Cuddles. You'll find her soon."

"What?" Casper froze. "How did you know?"

"Haven't you seen the note?" She lifted her hand to her mouth. "Oh, I'm so sorry."

"What note?"

"Come with me."

"But what about… OK." Casper turned back to Anemonie. "I'm not finished with you. I know you're not telling me something."

"Big deal, Cassie," sneered Anemonie. "Too bad I got nothing to tell you."

"Come on." Daisy took hold of Casper's hand and led him through the jungle of detectives. She felt calm and comforting, smoothing away

Casper's worries just for a moment. Lamp, still weighed down by the Bluff Boiler, scurried to catch up and took her other hand.

Daisy looked into Casper's eyes. "You sure you're fine?" she asked. "What about Cuddles?"

"Just a bit scared."

"Me too," piped Lamp. "I'm more scared, Daisy."

Daisy smiled sympathetically.

"You still haven't told me how you know," started Casper.

"Here."

The crowd was most dense and volatile by the vault door, where useless sleuths and village idiots clambered over each other to get a good view. But as soon as they spotted Casper, silence fell and the masses parted to let him through like a less wet and more idiotic Red Sea. He trod towards the door, flanked by Lamp and Daisy, past the ranks of whispering villagers on either side.

"That's him, the blonde one," said tiny Mitch McMassive, pointing his baby-sized finger up at Casper.

"Where?" warbled Mrs Trimble, the cat lady, fumbling in her bag of cats for a pair of spectacles.

"Ooh, he's not going to like this," hissed Audrey Snugglepuss.

On the door was nailed an elegantly scribed note on thick white card. Hundreds of unblinking eyes watched Casper as he unhooked it and read the inscription. What it said made the colour drain from his face like cheap fake tan in the rain.

*Mes amis*
*I have the biting baby.*
*I'll give it back,*
*But only for free passage out*
*of Corne-on-the-Kobb.*
*And I keep the sword.*
*A bientôt*

Casper felt sick. He ran a hand through his hair and grimaced. "Well," he said, "we'd better let the sword go."

The villagers gasped and Clemmie Answorth burst into tears.

"No chance," scoffed Sandy Landscape, adjusting his grubby hat. "I need my twenny-thousand smackers."

"But what about Cuddles?"

"It's only a baby," squeaked Mitch McMassive. "You can buy another one."

"And a nightmare of a baby, at that." Audrey Snugglepuss brandished the stump of what was once her left thumb but had recently been Cuddles' afternoon snack. A dozen other villagers murmured their agreement, pointing at their own plasters and bandages for proof.

"You can't do this!" shouted Casper, voice filled with desperation.

"She's a human being! She's my sister!"

Sandy Landscape tutted and shook his head. "Whatever she are, she ain't worth twenny grand."

There was a rousing round of applause and cries of "Well done" in support of Sandy's argument.

"So it's sorted," announced Mayor Rattsbulge,

hopping from leg to leg, anxious to get home for brunchfast (the meal between breakfast and brunch). "We leave the baby and find the sword."

The villagers cheered.

Casper gasped.

Lamp sneezed.

It was done. Casper stood there numbly, utterly defeated. The idiots gradually shuffled away, warbling cheerily about biscuits or cricket, or snooping in other people's handbags for the stolen sword.

Audrey Snugglepuss trotted over and waggled her bandaged thumb in Casper's face. "Good riddance."

A hot fog of anger bubbled up within Casper. He clenched his fists, furious at the mutton-headed villagers.

Daisy placed a hand on Casper's shoulder. "Don't let them get to you," she said coolly. "They're idiots."

"Is not French." A blackened finger prodded the card in Casper's hand.

Casper jumped from his skin and spun round. The blackened finger belonged to that odd little Frenchman from the day before, standing with his legs apart, sucking on a matchstick cigarette behind his faded beret.

"I'm sorry?"

"*Le Chat* – 'e is not French." A strong Gallic accent curled lazily from his phlegm-encrusted throat. "Zis –" he pointed to the 'A' of *A Bientôt* – "it should be 'À', not 'A'." He drew a downward dash over the 'A' with the ash from his cigarette. "You see? *À Bientôt*. 'À'.

Not 'A', 'À'."

"Ah," said Casper.

"Is not French," he repeated, then he stubbed out his cigarette and trudged away.

"Casper," said Lamp.

"Not now."

"No, Casper. It's important."

"What?" said Casper roughly, turning to face Lamp.

"The egg," he said. "It's hard-boiled. Someone's been lying."

## Chapter 9

# House Calls

The detectives had accidentally handcuffed themselves together into a big idiotic jumble at the other end of the village square, finally giving Casper, Lamp and Daisy some space to think.

"What do you make of that, then?" said Casper.

Lamp licked his lips. "Egg mayonnaise?"

"It must be Anemonie. She said she didn't know anything, but she's acting so shifty. And those scratches on her arm…"

"What about them?"

"I've seen them before." Casper held out his

arms, covered in exactly the same sorts of marks. There were bites and scratches of every size. He had a bruise on his upper left arm that was so purple and so round Casper's mum thought he'd got a tattoo of a plum. "Look!" he said, his face lighting up with excitement.

"At what?" said Lamp.

"I look after Cuddles, and this is the result. If Anemonie's all covered in bite marks, then she must have the baby."

Lamp wiggled and clapped his hands. "Let's get her."

"Hang on," said Daisy, "that doesn't prove anything. Watch. Yoo hoo, Mrs Trimble!" She waved at the old woman doddering across the square dragging a pack of cats on leads behind her.

"Oh, hello, love," warbled Mrs Trimble. (She

called everyone 'love', not because they were lovely, but because she was as blind as a bat.) "I didn't notice you there. Have you seen my Tiddles?"

"They're behind you," said Daisy, suppressing a giggle.

Mrs Trimble tugged on the leads, heard a chorus of strangled meows and smiled. "Oh, no, not them.

Look." She held up one lead that wasn't attached to a cat. "Now, unless I'm seeing things," – she wasn't; she never saw things – "this one hasn't got a Tiddles on it."

Daisy frowned. "No, you're right. But I'm afraid I haven't seen him."

"Ah well, he always turns up."

"Could you possibly show us your arms, please, Mrs Trimble?"

"What? Oh, all right," She rolled up one sleeve of her woolly jumper. Immediately one of the cats leapt on to her arm and started sharpening its claws on her rubbery skin. Mrs Trimble smiled vacantly at Daisy and patted the cat's head. "There's a good boy, Tiddles," she sang, and off she wandered, dragging the cats after her.

"You see?" said Daisy. "She had scratches all

over her arms."

"Well then, she's got Cuddles." Lamp clicked his fingers and started in her direction.

"No, Lamp." Daisy grabbed the neck of his boiler suit before he got away and tugged him back. "I'm just saying that we can't jump to conclusions."

"I love you," said Lamp, staring into Daisy's soft green eyes.

There was an awkward pause. Lamp had a bite of his boiled egg.

"Suppose you're right, Daisy," said Casper, hastily filling the gap. "It's just that Anemonie does all the evil stuff around here. And anyway, it fits. We know *Le Chat*'s going to have scratches, we know she's a she, and—"

"Do we?" Daisy sounded surprised. "How?"

"We… err… oh, dear." Casper knew he'd

rumbled himself. He'd have to tell her now. "We went looking for *Le Chat* last night. We found him, I mean her, but she stole Cuddles."

Daisy took a minute to take it all in. "But… that's great! You mean you've seen *Le Chat*? Why didn't you tell me?"

"We didn't want everyone to know we broke the curfew."

"I'm not everyone, Casper," Daisy smiled comfortingly. "You can trust me. So what did she look like?"

"It was very dark, but she's definitely a lady. We didn't see much more than that."

"Oh, well, it's a start. Now we don't have to bother about questioning the men."

"S'pose so," said Casper.

Daisy flicked back her hair. "All we need to do

is interview every woman we can find, look for scratches and see whose story doesn't match up. Lamp, we'll use your Bluff Boiler to check who's lying. Then we'll find the culprit, retrieve Cuddles and the sword and be home for dinner."

Lamp grinned at Daisy. "I love dinner."

"Still think it's Anemonie, though," said Casper.

Daisy shook her head. "Even if it is, we've got to run a full investigation. Let's do this properly, Casper."

"OK. But first we're going to need some more eggs."

So the three set off on their investigation, via Lamp's garage for another couple of dozen eggs. The sun rose higher in the sky, sweat sprang from boiling brows, and the backs of their necks scorched like frazzled bacon. But they had a job to do. Casper asked the questions, Daisy looked for scratches and Lamp was in charge of the eggs. Progress was as slow as the day was hot, and Lamp kept dodging from shadow to shadow and asking for a sit-down. They tramped from house to house, Bluff Boiler whirring away, interviewing every female they found. They'd thank them kindly, bid them goodbye and then crack the Bluff-Boiled eggs on the front gate to check for fibs. This is what they found:

- Clemmie Answorth was grazed and bruised all down one side. However, she makes a habit of falling off chairs, horses and aeroplanes, and thus collects bruises like Audrey Snugglepuss collects speeding fines. She spent yesterday evening at the bottom of a well after

losing her balance when making a wish. As they left, Clemmie demonstrated her clumsiness by falling out of a window. Her egg was raw.

- Joan Oatcakes' clothes were in tatters, but she put this down to the family of ravenous clothes' moths staying in her spare room. Casper suggested mothballs, but Joan said she was a vegetarian. Her evening had been spent in the spare room with a fly swatter and a moth cloth. Her egg was also raw.

- Amanda Candlewacks was found digging up her front garden, still losing at hide-and-seek and (understandably, for Cuddles's mother) covered in

Cuddly wounds. This made Lamp very suspicious, but Casper reminded him of the family connection. They decided not to tell her about the ransom note, as her poor nerves wouldn't take it. Yet again, the egg was raw.

• Village gossip Audrey Snugglepuss had a black eye and a couple of missing teeth. She'd "fallen over dozens of times looking for that stupid sword in the dark the night it was stolen, thank you very much". She also mentioned that she despised Cuddles and wouldn't let that little rat anywhere near her antique collection of speeding fines – so it couldn't have been her. Lamp thought that because her name had 'puss' in it, she was a very likely suspect for a cat burglar. Her egg, however, was raw.

• Sandra Landscape (Sandy's wife) kept a hive of biting bees that require constant supervision and tooth-clipping. Raw.

• Bernice Sideboard's rugby match had turned ugly, but not as ugly as Bernice was, all covered in stud marks and rugby-ball-shaped bruises. Raw.

• Marjorie Mildew had had a painful encounter with a faulty set of battery-powered dentures, for which Lamp apologised and offered to make her some more. Raw, raw, raw.

As the baking sun melted into afternoon, Casper, Daisy and Lamp approached the final house of the village – Blight Manor. It stood alone at the end of Long Lost Drive, set apart from its neighbouring houses like the smelly man on a bus. A gravel path curled up through browned lawns to a looming, decrepit mansion with crumbling grey walls and mainly boarded-up windows. Black and rotten ivy drooped languidly from the stone buttresses, overlooking a gnarled tree stump sitting sullenly amongst a patch of bristling gorse. There was no birdsong, no flowers and the air was colder. Casper felt a shiver run down his spine.

"Who lives here then?" Daisy felt the need to whisper.

"Anemonie," chorused the boys.

The three of them crunched timidly up the broad drive, each experiencing that tingling sensation you get when being watched. Sure enough, Casper peered up to a second-floor window and flinched as he caught sight of the sharp skeletal face of Anemonie Blight. She squinted menacingly at Casper and then darted back into the shadows.

"Lamp, get the Bluff Boiler started," said Casper.

With a trembling hand, Lamp placed his last egg on the Bluff Boiler's dish and gulped. "Can we go home now?"

At about fifteen paces from the house, the great black door creaked open and the imposing gaunt figure of Mrs Blight stepped out from the darkness, scowling like a razor-beaked vulture. She wore all black save for a heavy swab of violet lipstick on her pursed lips, matching the bulbous purple wart on her pointy nose. "Take your business elsewhere, Candlewacks." She stepped out fully on to the porch and closed the door behind her.

"We just want to ask you some questions, Mrs Blight; that's all," Casper gulped.

"Not interested. Get off my drive." She inspected her three visitors through narrowed eyes, and then with a silent laugh her glare settled on Daisy. "Helping them solve the case, Miss Blossom?"

"We-we just want to know where you were last night," Daisy stammered.

"Why, what happened last night?" Mrs Blight's purple lips curled into a daring smile.

"*Le Chat* stole Cuddles."

Her eyes swept towards Casper. "And Cuddles was tucked up in bed, was she?"

That look she was giving him… she knew about last night! But Casper couldn't lie or he'd boil the egg no matter what she said. "Where else would she be?" he answered more bravely than he felt.

"Oh, I don't know. It just seems strange that *Le Chat* would come all the way to—"

"You're *Le Chat*, aren't you?" Casper's blood pounded, his courage returning.

"Of course I'm not," Mrs Blight simpered. "And neither's my Nemmie, before you ask."

Casper's skin prickled. "We know you've got Cuddles."

"You think you know everything, little boy." Mrs Blight wrinkled her nose. "Well, you don't. I'm not *Le Chat*, but might I suggest you look a little closer to home?" With a sweep of her jet-black dress she whisked round and strode back into her house, slamming the door behind her.

"I hate that woman." Casper's face was still crimson with anger.

"Me too," said Daisy, deep in thought.

"Ooh! The Bluff Boiler." Lamp grasped the egg and cracked it on the side of the pan. A slimy glob of white dribbled down and dripped to the floor. "It's raw," he said, eyes wide.

"But…" Casper searched for more words to say, but they were all hiding.

"So it's not the Blights?" said Daisy.

"Can't be," said Lamp. "My Bluff Boiler works perfectly."

Casper clutched his head. Every egg had come out raw. The whole village was telling the truth and nobody was *Le Chat*. "What now?"

Daisy shrugged. "Time for tea?"

## Chapter 10

# Tea at the Blossoms'

Casper flicked a straggle of sweaty hair out of his face and fanned himself with a hand. "So we've lost. We don't know who it is."

Daisy looked worried. "It has to be someone. We'll ask around again tomorrow, OK?"

"I was *so sure* it was Anemonie or her mum."

Lamp was scuttling behind, desperate to catch up. "Daisy, Daisy, I made you a present." He proudly handed her a leftover boiled egg.

"That's beautiful, thank you." Daisy smiled

and took the egg, holding it awkwardly with two fingers. "I'll save it for later."

Lamp grinned and adjusted his boiler suit.

It was late afternoon, but the scorching day had hardly cooled. The village seemed to sag under the stifling heat like an old mattress. Casper's investigation had been as unsuccessful as the day was hot, and he hoped never to see another egg again in his life.

"Hello there, sonny Jim. Found us that sword yet?" The willowy figure of Headlock Bones clambered out of a bush in Betty Woons's front garden and strutted into the road to block their path.

With a grunt and a rustle of leaves, his burly sidekick, Wartson, tumbled out after him, covered in mud and sticks and a disgruntled grasshopper.

Lamp clung to Daisy's arm. "Who are those

men and what were they doing in that bush?" he asked a little bit too loudly.

"They're bullies," said Casper.

"Oh, we're worse than that. We're your worst nightmare, sonny Jim." Headlock Bones's lip curled as he doffed his deerstalker hat at Lamp.

"My name's actually Lamp, sir, not Jim."

"I know what your name is. We've been following you all day."

Lamp gulped.

"Now," – he took his time, drawing slowly on his pipe – "who's going to tell me where I can find that sword?"

"We don't have it." Casper's voice came out all quavery.

"Oh, I'm quite confident you don't. But you're getting close, aren't you?"

"What about my hat, boss?" snarled Wartson, waving around the flattened black cloth that used to be his bowler hat. "I sat on it in the bush."

"Oh, Wartson, what a shame." Headlock Bones's eyes narrowed. "I bet one of these chaps could lend you a shilling for a new one."

Wartson turned to face Casper with a rotten-toothed grin. "Gimme your money or I'll thump ya." His knuckles cracked threateningly.

"Haven't got any." Casper stepped back, trembling.

"Don't lie." Wartson crunched forward. "What's in those pockets?"

Daisy jumped into Wartson's path and struck a frosty face. "Leave us alone."

Wartson faltered. Nobody had spoken to him like that since Mash-faced Mick back in '86 (and we all know what happened to him). With a snarl Wartson raised his clenched fist, but Daisy met his glare.

"You wouldn't *dare* hit a girl."

Stunned, Wartson dropped his fist. He blinked, then stumbled backwards.

"Thought not." Daisy strutted straight between the two men, followed by the two dumbfounded boys.

Moments later the spell broke. "Oy!" roared Headlock Bones. "Come back here, you scallywags!"

"Run!" Daisy led the three as they sprinted towards the square, hotly pursued by Bones and Wartson.

"How'd you do that?" Casper gasped, trying to keep pace with Daisy.

"Doesn't matter right now. Just keep running."

Hundreds of detectives stood in the square, watching vacantly as the three children dashed towards Blossom's Bloomers.

"HEY, EVERYONE," bellowed Terry, smashing two windows and deafening a pigeon, "SUSPECTS!"

A stampede of idiots armed with magnifying glasses turned, gasped and trampled across the square in Casper's direction.

"We've got trouble," groaned Daisy.

The herd grew closer, gathering speed as it went.

"I'm too young to be squashed," Lamp's voice trembled.

The oncoming idiot storm was only metres away now. Casper's eyes darted around, looking for an escape. Then, just at that moment, Headlock

Bones and Wartson marched into the square, red-faced and furious.

"Look!" Casper yelled, "There's *Le Chat*!"

The herd screamed and swerved towards the newcomers, stampeding away from the three and brushing past Lamp's shoulder with only a few centimetres to spare.

Headlock Bones and Wartson stopped in their tracks, terrified. The clueless amateur detectives charged towards them, and now they'd gathered momentum they didn't look much like stopping. Headlock Bones's jaw fell open, his pipe clattering to the ground. He tried to shield himself behind Wartson, but found only fresh air – his gallant henchman was already halfway back down the road, screaming like a black pudding in a vampire novel. Headlock took one more look at the advancing sleuth army and scarpered in the same direction as his friend. The herd disappeared after them, yelling nonsensical war cries and lobbing hopeful pairs of handcuffs.

Within the blink of an eye the square was empty except for Casper, Lamp and Daisy, and a deaf pigeon wondering where his new friends had gone.

"Wow." Lamp wiped his brow. "That was close."

Casper laughed. "Got rid of both our problems, though, didn't it?"

With the coast clear, Daisy led the boys into Blossom's Bloomers. Through a door at the back of the shop was a dingy corridor, and this took them out, blinking, into a conservatory so impossibly beautiful that Casper had to pinch himself – and even that didn't convince him.

A breathtaking array of vibrant and tropical plants climbed from floor to ceiling, weaving in and out of each other like green spaghetti and bursting into bloom wherever they could. The early evening light streamed in through the glass roof, bathing the foliage in a warm golden glow. Casper's nostrils were bombarded by the fragrant cocktail of sweet nectars and petals; his ears were serenaded by the tuneful twitterings of tiny birds. In the centre of the room stood a trestle table, wrought-iron legs entwined with creepers, and four chairs, one occupied by the ravishingly beautiful Lavender Blossom.

"Come on in, for goodness' sake," she sang, patting the chair next to her. "What's all that commotion out there, anyway?"

"You'll never believe us," chuckled Daisy,

picking pigeon feathers from her hair.

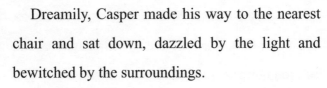

Dreamily, Casper made his way to the nearest chair and sat down, dazzled by the light and bewitched by the surroundings.

Lamp plonked himself on the next chair with his mouth agape. Steadily, he leant towards Casper and whispered, "Is this heaven?"

Casper shrugged.

"Mum, we've been investigating."

"Really?" Lavender's eyes twinkled as she laughed. "Who's the culprit, then?"

"I wish I knew," said Casper.

"Ah, me too. I've had people at my door all day, and none of them have a clue. If you work it out, you're a brighter spark than I am, Casper."

"Well," he blushed. "It's just that…" He didn't mean to tell her anything, but before he could stop himself the whole story tumbled out like a mouthful of baby squirrels, with the occasional pause for breath while Lamp interjected with his own side of the tale. Meanwhile, Daisy had slipped off for a moment and reappeared with a large primrose teapot filled with chamomile tea. She poured out four cups, stirred each with a teaspoon of honey and passed them round the table. Then there was sponge cake, apricot brownies and sweet walnut loaf with generous dollops of raspberry jam. Lavender listened intently, nodding and laughing gracefully, placing a motherly hand on Casper's during the sad bits.

"…So basically, we don't know." By the time Casper had finished his story he was full to bursting and exhausted, and Lamp had fallen asleep on his shoulder.

"Well," chuckled Lavender, "no wonder he's tired."

Casper looked at his watch. Six o'clock. "Poor Mum. I haven't told her what happened. She still thinks it's a game of hide-and-seek."

Lavender lent Casper a second comforting hand. "Break it to her gently. Goodness knows how I'd feel if I lost my Daisy."

Casper sighed. "I don't even want the sword any more, if it means getting Cuddles back."

"You're right," said Lavender. "One sword's worth nothing compared to your baby sister. The villagers should agree to *Le Chat*'s terms if they have an ounce of sense."

"But all they want is their sword. They're all scared of Cuddles."

"You have to convince them. Show them you

need your sister back. They can't hold out for ever, Casper."

"You don't understand – nobody listens to me."

"Well, they should. You make more sense than the rest of this village put together. So you think they'll never agree to *Le Chat*'s demands? Hmm." Lavender reached across for a brownie, but her sleeve caught on the edge of the table, revealing a fine set of scratches on her wrist. Casper caught his breath and pretended not to notice, but Daisy had spotted his reaction.

"Oh, don't worry about those. We've had a new delivery of Venus Flytraps, but we just can't tame them."

Lavender nodded sagely. "Awful biters, the lot of them." She swivelled on her chair and lifted a red earthenware pot on to the table. "Here's one."

Casper shuddered at the sight of the monstrous plant. A thick green stalk led up to two gigantic

leaves, each with a row of pink needley teeth slowly chewing the air. Daisy cut a corner off her walnut loaf and popped it into the Venus Flytrap's mouth. It snapped shut with a *Glomp!* and the loaf was gone, save for one sanguine trickle of raspberry jam running down the stalk.

"You're supposed to wear gloves." Lavender lifted the pot back to its place on the floor and brushed off her hands. "We'll soon have them house-trained."

Lamp awoke and yawned, a trail of dribble stringing lazily over his chin.

"Oh." He looked around, wide-eyed, and blinked. "I thought this was a dream." Daisy giggled, which made him giggle too.

Lavender clasped her hands together. "Well then, shall we dance away all our troubles at the Summer Ball tonight?"

Casper shook his head. "I hadn't even thought of going."

"I'm going with Daisy," announced Lamp.

"Are you?" asked Casper.

"Are you?" asked Daisy.

"Yes, of course. I've made a new costume."

"All right," replied Daisy, grinning, "but only if Casper goes." She stole a quick glance in his direction.

Casper grimaced. "Not while Cuddles is…"

"Come on, it'll be fun."

"No, I'm not going. I can't dance."

"I can dance," said Lamp, eagerly turning to Daisy. (Lamp really couldn't dance. After his disastrous attempt at a can-can in last year's school disco they had to build a new assembly hall.)

A *meow* from within the foliage distracted Casper from his worries.

"Weird," he muttered. "What flower makes that noise?"

Daisy shrugged. "Catkins?"

*Meow*. There it was again, followed by an

infernal crash as a large clay pot toppled to the floor and shattered. Then out from behind a vine blundered a large ginger-and-black tomcat, teetering from side to side and howling miserably.

"Here, kitty," Lamp held out a hand, but when the cat stepped forward for a rub he missed it by miles and keeled over sideways. "What's he doing?"

Lavender's brow furrowed. "We get a lot of strays in here. I think they like the plants."

The cat rolled around on the floor before finally managing to wobble to its feet. Casper caught a look at its collar and gasped. "That's not a stray. It's Tiddles – Mrs Trimble's lost cat."

Daisy clapped her hands with delight. "We've found him! She'll be so happy." She whistled at Tiddles and he stumbled towards her, but he veered off course and bonked headfirst into a table leg. Flopping to a sitting position, he looked glumly at Casper and howled.

"Something's wrong with him." Casper scratched Tiddles behind the ear with his finger.

"Maybe he's broken," said Lamp, rooting around in his pocket for a screwdriver. "I'll have a look."

"No, Lamp. You'll hurt him."

"He might just need an oil change."

"Cats don't use any oil."

"Well, that's probably the problem, isn't it."

"Now now, Lamp," cooed Lavender. "That's not how we treat cats. Come on, Tiddles, let's get you home." She reached down to whisk him away from Lamp's screwdriver, but he hissed like a gas leak, puffed up his tail and bolted out of the room, only missing a faceful of doorframe by the width of a gremlin's eyebrow (eight millimetres, if you're acting it out at home). He scrabbled down the hallway, thudding into something thuddy, clanging into something clangy, then bursting through the shop's front door and out into the deserted square.

"Odd." Casper didn't really understand animals – the closest thing he'd ever had to a pet was Cuddles – but he couldn't help thinking there was something seriously wrong with Tiddles. "Should we go after him?"

"No." Lavender's soft voice carried a waver of worry. "He'll find his way home. Cats are very good with directions."

"He wasn't." Tiddles' appearance had broken

175

the spell for Casper, and as the sun went behind a cloud he found himself restless, his thoughts drawn once more to Cuddles and Amanda. "I'd better get home." Casper pushed back his chair and brushed the crumbs from his lap. Lamp crammed in a last mouthful of cake and joined him, still grinning at Daisy through jammy teeth, and they made their way to the front of the shop, thanking the Blossoms for the tea and cake and anything else that came to mind.

The empty square was strewn with crushed flowers, smashed magnifying glasses and crumpled notebooks scrawled with pea-brained theories such as 'Sneaky-looking pigeon on roof – enquire further!' and 'Murder weapon was a flannel!' Lamp accompanied the walk home with a jolly song about Daisy, but it petered out in the

second verse when he ran out of words that he knew. He trotted along in silence for a while, but then he noticed Casper's frown. "Why's your face all crumpled?"

"Nothing. Just the way Tiddles looked at me. I feel like I'm missing something." But the something didn't come. Casper's head was a noisy jumble sale of cluttered worries, cats, boiled eggs and big bejewelled swords. He didn't notice Lamp wave goodbye at the Feete Street postbox, or the pile of snoozing detectives on the corner of Cracklin' Crescent. Casper's mind was elsewhere, sifting through the chaos in his brain and longing for a nap.

## Chapter 11

# Grounded

Amanda Candlewacks was banging around in the attic when Casper arrived home. Judging by the absence of floorboards, she was still hard at her game of hide-and-seek.

Julius looked too exhausted to embark on any new hair-brained projects. Instead he sat slouched in the living room yelling at some lizards in a nature documentary.

Traipsing into the kitchen, Casper brewed himself a cup of tea (white, four sugars) and one for his mum (black, eight sugars), and crossed his fingers (white, no sugars). Then he made his way upstairs.

"Brought you some tea, Mum," he said, climbing the final few steps to the attic.

"Did you check in the mug for Cuddles?" Amanda sat amongst a grubby pile of floorboards with a hammer in one hand and the poster of Tiddles in the other, head smothered with dust.

"I've got something to tell you."

"You know where she is?" Amanda sat bolt upright, eyes wide.

"Sort of."

"Ooh! Tell me, tell me!" In the process of scrabbling forward, Amanda knocked over both cups of tea, which seeped through the floorboards and gave a family of rats a hot shower.

"Well," Casper gulped. Telling Lavender had been easy, so why not Mum? She knelt in front of him, her eyes keen, her mouth slightly open. With fingers firmly crossed, Casper began.

"I wanted to catch *Le Chat* for the reward money for Dad's restaurant so Lamp and I went to the crime scene last night and I took Cuddles because I thought she could sniff for clues, and we saw *Le Chat*, but Cuddles chased after her and they both disappeared before we got there and then there was a note from *Le Chat* saying she'd give Cuddles back if we let her leave with the sword, but the villagers don't even want Cuddles, so we spent the day looking for her instead." He collapsed on to the banister and gasped in most of the air in the attic. "But I'll find her," he blurted, "I promise." He tried to swallow, but his mouth was bone dry.

There was a long pause, during which a tea-stained rat scuttled out from the floorboards looking for a biscuit to dunk.

Eventually Amanda muttered, "So she's not playing hide-and-seek?"

"No."

"Not even one round?"

"Not even one round."

"But I didn't look inside the pillows."

"She's not inside the pillows, Mum." Casper reached a hand towards her, but she snapped it away. "I've been looking for her all day."

"Me too." She clambered to her feet and shuffled numbly past Casper down the stairs. "And it was fun till you turned up."

"I'll find her, Mum. I will," he yelled, scrambling after her.

Amanda looked at Casper, blank-faced and expressionless. "How can you find her? You told me yourself – she's not even playing hide-and-seek." She turned away, sniffed and shuffled down the second flight of stairs, still frantically pursued by Casper.

"It doesn't matter about the game, I'll look for her anyway."

"No, you won't. You're grounded. You're not leaving this house until you've put all these floorboards back down and fixed the kitchen window." Arriving in the dingy living room, Amanda plonked herself on the sofa next to Julius and stared at the TV screen.

"Mum," Casper shouted. "Mum!"

No answer. A cheer rose from the telly as a group of tap-dancing nuns made it through to the semi-finals of *Convent Idol.*

"Mum, listen to me."

The nuns began a victory performance. *Clickity clickity clack clack clack.*

"Dad."

*Clickity clickity clack.* "*Alleluia!*"

"I'll find Cuddles. I promise."

*Clomp clomp clomp clack.* "*Amen!*"

"Listen to me!"

A round of applause, then a bear advertising socks.

Bursting with frustration, Casper stomped up the stairs to his room and threw himself face down on to the bed. Before he could help it, salty tears pushed themselves through and dribbled down his face, making little damp patches on the pillow. "I will, I will," he cried. "I will find you, Cuddles."

Then the tears flooded through and he sobbed like he was five again, squeezing the pillow and gritting his teeth. He sobbed and sobbed until, eventually, he could sob no more.

By now the room was dark and stuffy and it smelt of curried feet. Casper lay motionless on his bed, eyes unblinking. His mind flitted from place to place; first to Cuddles, then Lamp and Daisy, and then to the Summer Ball, which made him smile feebly. *At least I don't have to go and dance*, he thought. The other two would have such fun together clowning around on the dance floor. Everyone would be there, twirling and prancing and spilling their wine. Well, not everyone. Not Cuddles.

"Hang on," Casper leapt out of bed and landed on a plastic truck. "OUCH." He grabbed his foot, hopping around the room in a mixture of agony and enlightenment. "Not Cuddles!" Of course Cuddles wouldn't be there – she'd been kidnapped. But leave her alone for thirty seconds, even in a cage made of bite-proof galvanised super-steel surrounded by a pack of grouchy tigers with poisoned claws, and Cuddles would gnaw her way out with time left for a glass of milk and a quick nap. In other words, if *Le Chat* didn't want Cuddles to bite her house down, she'd have to be guarded full-time. "And that leaves no time to go to the ball. So whoever doesn't come… is *Le Chat*!" Casper clapped his hands and leapt from the other end of the room to his bed. "I can find out who it is! I have to go to the ball."

"You *shall* go to the ball," sang the Fairy Godmother, appearing from nowhere with a sparkle. Oh… hang on; wrong story.

Then it struck him like a muddy spade to the face. "Oh no. Mum, and the floorboards. I can't leave the house." As instantly as it had arrived, the excitement poured out of Casper and left him furry-tongued and punctured. There was no way out: to get to the front or the back door meant walking right past the living room. Amanda would see him, and that would spell the end of it. Rubbing his temples pensively, Casper took a slow breath. "OK, Casper, think." He paced round the edge of his room, looking for an answer. What would a superhero do? "Fly, I suppose." He laughed emptily and flung open the window. A long way down. "I'd be too scared to fly, anyway."

Then, out of the corner of his eye he spotted the sturdy metal drainpipe stretching from the roof, past his window, right down to a prickly hawthorn bush in the garden.

Casper chuckled. "I couldn't."

The pipe glinted temptingly.

"Could I?"

It was perfectly strong, securely attached to the wall.

"How hard could it be?" Marvelling at his own idiocy, he scrambled for the tin can and rasped, "Lamp."

There was some clucking, a giggle and then, "Hullo, Casper."

"We can solve this tonight just by going to the ball. See you outside your garage in five minutes."

"Just wait till you see my costume." With an eager squeak Lamp shuffled away and the tin can fell silent.

He'd never done this before – daring escapes only happened in books. But there was the drainpipe, easily within stretching distance. He clambered on to the sill and grasped the pipe with his right hand, then eased himself fully out, clinging on with gritty determination and gripping the pipe with his legs like a circus monkey. This was Casper's third window escape in 24 hours, but no matter now many times he did it he'd always prefer the less dramatic door option. Centimetre by centimetre he shinned down the pipe, praying that his clammy hands didn't squeak on the metal. He descended gingerly, palms stinging. Then his foot accidentally kicked the back living-room window, only metres away from his parents. Casper grimaced. If they turned round now he'd be caught, no question, but they didn't stir, mesmerised as they were by *America's Top Possum.* How much further? He dared to peek at the remaining drop. Halfway, thank goodness. But in looking down, his left hand slipped from the pipe, his right couldn't take the weight and Casper found himself swiping at cold air as he flipped backwards from the pipe and crashed heavily into the spiky embrace of a hawthorn bush. He cried out through gritted teeth as prickles impaled him like a pincushion, but he wrestled free and ducked below the window before his parents could tear their eyes from the screen. Casper bit his knuckles and counted to five. Nobody stirred. Holding his breath, he crawled on all fours to the side gate, unlatched it and scampered through to freedom.

Exhilarated yet perforated, Casper hobbled the

distance to Lamp's, wincing at every step. Little scarlet pinpricks punctuated his faded T-shirt like full stops of pain (which were great for livening up old clothes, but terrible at ending sentences). The deed was done – he'd defied his mother's orders, so failure to find Cuddles tonight would be disastrous. But the task was simple – spot who wasn't at the ball, sneak out and head for their house, then catch the culprit and retrieve Cuddles along with the sword. Simple, foolproof and— "Lamp, what on earth are you wearing?"

Lamp stood proudly in front of his garage, hands on hips, covered from head to toe in a thick mat of white feathers. He ran on the spot, flapping his wings and yelling, "My costume, Casper. Guess what it's made of?"

Mavis and Bessie cowered naked and shivering

behind Lamp, watching their feathered friend with envy.

Lamp patted the hens' heads. "The ladies lent me their feathers. I'll give them back tomorrow."

"It's not fancy dress," Casper grimaced.

"Course it is." Lamp frowned at Casper's outfit. "Who are you going as?"

"Nobody. Just me."

"Doesn't look anything like you. What's all the blood for?"

Casper brushed down his crimson-specked T-shirt.

"I've got some spare feathers if you want," Lamp continued.

"No, thanks."

Mavis clucked rudely.

"Anyway, we've got a cat burglar to catch."

Lamp's face dropped. "What about the ball?"

"We're still going, but we might need to slip out."

"As long as I get to dance with Daisy," Lamp grinned. "Do you think she'll like my costume?"

## Chapter 12

# The Funky Chicken

Mayor Rattsbulge squished his greasy nose against the window, his bloated stomach rumbling at the sight of the buffet table piled high with the crispiest sausage rolls since records began. "You're mine, you golden beauties," he rumbled, licking the spittle from his drooping lips.

Half an hour ago tiny Mitch McMassive had clambered on to the back of Bean, the pub dog, and galloped about the village, rounding up the detectives and herding them into the village hall. He ankle-cuffed them in position and now, squawking with resentment, they poured drinks, blew up balloons or manned the cloakroom. Terry had got hold of the microphone and was acting as master of ceremonies, to the dismay of anybody with ears.

Behind the mayor in the queue outside muddled the rest of the early arrivals, dressed in silky frocks and pretty bonnets, gaggling like geese.

"Don't you look just ravishing, love," warbled Mrs Trimble to Clemmie Answorth, who'd put her dress on the wrong way up.

"Oh, nothing compared to you," replied Clemmie, gesturing at Mrs Trimble's squirming black scarf. "But why's it moving?"

"It's all made of Tiddleses." The scarf unwound itself from Mrs Trimble's neck and meowed. "Very warm."

Mrs Trimble's cat-scarf jabbed a claw at Clemmie, who screamed and fell backwards over Mitch McMassive into a flowerbed.

The boys joined the back of the queue behind Sandy Landscape, who had brushed his teeth *and* polished his wellies for the occasion. Casper impatiently tapped his feet, counting heads to see who was missing.

"See, it *is* fancy dress." Lamp pointed his wing at Sandy. "He's come as a gardener."

"He *is* a gardener," Casper whispered.

"But he's come as a mayor, and she's come as a lady, and… Ooh! The queue's moving." Lamp's excitement bubbled over and he did a little jig on the spot.

The moment the clock struck eight, Mayor Rattsbulge threw open the doors and thundered

towards the buffet table with a ravenous squeal, trampling straight over the ticket-collecting sleuth. The rest of the villagers roared in behind him, flattening the already pancake-thin ticket-collector to the thickness of tracing paper. The hall was gaily decked out with flowery bunting provided by Lavender Blossom and a large white bedsheet was taped to the rafters on which Sandy Landscape had daubed Hapey Sumer, in messy red letters. He kept nudging people and pointing up at it, nodding sagely and saying, "It were I what made that, it were."

Casper counted the villagers through the door on his fingers from a seat in the corner. Next to him Lamp picked at his feathers impatiently.

Over in another corner, that ruddy-faced Frenchman sat sullenly sipping a large glass of red wine, watching the boys through the slits of his eyes.

"He's here again," groaned Casper.

"Oh, no," Lamp fluttered. "Is he looking at me? The French eat chickens."

"We eat chickens, Lamp. Everyone does."

"Do they?" He cowered back in his chair. "Everyone?"

"It's all right. You're not a real chicken."

"But *they* don't know that."

"Look, if anyone tries to eat you, just tell them who you are."

"Oh, OK then." Lamp practised saying his name for a bit.

Soon the hall was brim full of boisterous revellers bouncing around to the disco tunes, while Terry bellowed dance instructions into the microphone. Anemonie and her pointy mother hadn't arrived yet; neither had Daisy or Lavender, Audrey Snugglepuss or fourteen other villagers by Casper's estimate. But as time ticked on they seeped in.

First came Audrey and her cake-appreciating minions, booting children out of the way to make space for the gigantic carrot cake, carried on wooden struts and a huge silver platter. In scooted the previously cricket-batted Betty Woons, who was now zipping around the dance floor like a mummy in a wheelchair, bandages streaming behind her. Then came Daisy and Lavender, both in sparkly purple dresses with sweet-pea tiaras. Their arrival lit up the hall, prompting an adoring gasp from every man and an adoring clunk as Clemmie Answorth fell off her chair. Lamp squeaked and skipped towards Daisy.

Half past eight ticked by and Casper shifted awkwardly in his chair, heart pounding. A glass of neglected fruit punch sat next to him, trying to look as juicy as possible, but it was no use – Casper was concentrating far too hard to be thirsty. The only villagers missing now were burly brothers Baz and Gaz Laszlo, who were guarding the roads, the three other Candlewackses and the pointy-nosed Blights.

"It's Anemonie," Casper muttered. "It must be. But the Bluff Boiler said it wasn't, and it's been right every time. Hasn't it?"

Deep in the heaving dance floor Lamp stamped and clapped and rolled around, casting clouds of feathers in every direction and knocking Clemmie Answorth to the floor again, while Daisy, though sneezing, boogied along as best she could.

Mayor Rattsbulge wobbled over to the door with a sausage roll in one hand and a sausage roll in the other. "Curfew!" he yelled, spitting flaky crumbs all over some nearby revellers. "Nobody enters, nobody leaves." He slammed the door, stuffed one of the sausage rolls in his greasy chops and wobbled back to the buffet table before starvation set in.

"Lamp, Daisy," Casper struggled through the dance floor, trembling with excitement. "Anemonie's the enemy."

"What?" Daisy cupped her ear, straining to hear over the music.

Lamp had dropped to the floor and was spinning on his bum.

"It's Anemonie and her mum. They're *Le Chat*."

"Really?" she shouted, eyes wide. "But the Bluff Boiler—"

"I know. Follow me." Casper beckoned and fought his way off the dance floor.

Daisy followed, sliding Lamp along the floor behind her.

They found a quieter corner of the room, where there was space to breathe or think – perhaps even both (except in Lamp's case, obviously).

"Casper." Daisy looked worried.

"I'm sorry, Lamp, but your Bluff Boiler must've gone wrong. It is the Blights after all."

"No, Casper—" Daisy persisted.

"Listen, I've proved it."

"Have you, now?" Headlock Bones's mahogany pipe appeared from behind a pillar, as well as Headlock Bones's deerstalker hat, Headlock

Bones's navy-blue cravat and the rest of Headlock
Bones's vile self, along with his thuggish sidekick,
Wartson, munching on a stolen fistful of carrot cake.

Lamp gasped.

"Yes, sonny Jim. We're back. And this time
you're going nowhere." The two men edged
forward, blocking their three young captives in the
very corner of the hall.

Casper's heart dropped. "How did
you…?"

"Escape the stampede?" Bones's face
curled into a hateful grimace. "If you must
know, we hid up a tree."

Lamp giggled.

"Don't you *dare* laugh at me." Bones
grabbed Lamp's shoulder and twisted, and
Lamp's laugh turned to a howl of pain.

Fury coursed through Casper's veins. "Nobody hurts my friend!" He lunged at the two men, but Wartson held Casper back with one hand on his forehead, sniggering through a mouthful of cake. A sticky cloud of crumbs sprayed all over Casper's face.

Casper struggled, but Wartson was too strong. Exhausted, he let the brute shove him to the wall and he didn't try to get back up.

Lamp snuffled back the tears as Bones released him, burying his head in his feathers for comfort.

"Now," – Bones dusted off his gloved hands – "can we have some answers or will Wartson here have to make this a little less comfortable?"

Wartson cracked his knuckles.

Daisy scowled. "We don't know anything."

"I don't need a boiled egg to tell me that's a lie," smirked Bones. "Why, I even heard Blondie over there say he's proved it." He poked a finger at Casper. "What have you proved, sonny Jim?"

Casper shook his head.

"I said," Headlock's pipe began to tremble, "what have you proved?"

The brutes towered over Casper and his knees shook, but he swallowed his fear and said, "E equals MC squared."

"HOW DARE YOU!" roared Bones, stepping forward with hands raised to throttle Casper. But at that moment Daisy pronged two fingers into Wartson's eyes and he bent double, howling with agony.

Casper spotted his moment. Like a dart, he snatched Bones's pipe and dived through the gap between the two men. He landed on his hands and knees and scrabbled to the safety of the dance floor before Bones and Wartson could grab him. They forgot about Lamp and pursued Casper into the crowd, furiously knocking aside boogying villagers to clear a path. But Casper was far too nimble, slight enough to duck between the middle of a waltzing couple and twirl to the other side of the hall unseen.

At that moment from the sausage-roll table Mayor Rattsbulge announced, "Speech!" and the music stopped, the lights came on and Headlock and Wartson found themselves stranded in the middle of the dance floor surrounded by people who were absolutely not Casper Candlewacks.

"Now, there are some people I'd like to thank," Mayor Rattsbulge rumbled, "namely myself for providing the money for these sausage rolls; myself again for the venue; also myself for the marvellous music selection and for anything else I might have forgotten. Now, I have prepared a few words for the occasion…" He pulled out a scruffy piece of paper with a bite taken out of it and started droning on about community development and the re-introduction of the pie tax. But if he'd looked round, he might have seen a sneaky hand reach up behind his sausage-roll table and pilfer one of the greasy devils from the nearest plate, only to disappear a moment later.

"So for tonight, let's put the sword behind us, and get on with a right good party."

The crowd cheered and Mayor Rattsbulge

returned to his feast.

But just before Terry could stick the music back on again, the mayor interrupted. "HANG ON ONE TURKEY-BASTING MOMENT!"

All turned to face him once more.

"Sixty-nine." His jaw wobbled furiously. "Sixty-nine sausage rolls. I left seventy. Someone's stolen one!"

The crowd screamed.

"It's *Le Chat*," gasped Audrey Snugglepuss.

"He's back," swooned Clemmie Answorth.

"Found it!" The blonde head of Casper Candlewacks popped up behind the cloaked figures of Headlock Bones and Wartson, standing in the centre of the dance floor. "This man took your sausage roll, Mayor Rattsbulge," he said, pointing at Headlock.

"Is this true?" The mayor stomped towards him, cracking the fragile dance floor beneath his enormous feet.

"No, my man," Headlock trembled, "I swear, I'd never—"

"Check his pockets," said Casper.

The mayor stuffed a chubby hand into Headlock's coat pocket and withdrew it, shaking, with a golden pastry squeezed between his fingers.

"You... you thief!"

A ripple of excitement spread through the crowd.

"There's only one person capable of such unforgivable crimes..." Mayor Rattsbulge's jowls vibrated dangerously, "and that's *LE CHAT*! GET HIM!"

Casper danced between the flying bodies as

the entire population of Corne-on-the-Kobb leapt upon Headlock Bones. Wartson, never to miss out on a brawl, dived on top, while Lamp and Daisy watched from their corner with mouths agape.

"But…?" Daisy's mouth opened and closed, but the words were stuck in a traffic jam halfway up her windpipe.

"I put them there," grinned Casper. "Now, come on. We need to get out of here." He bundled Lamp and Daisy through the nearest open door and bolted it behind him.

The room that Casper found himself in was pitch-black, putrid and certainly too small for two children and a giant chicken. He was squished into a corner like a tinned sardine, his face pressed up against what tasted like Lamp's feathers, and his foot feeling worryingly soggy. Fumbling for a light switch, he found a cord and tugged it. It flushed.

"We're in the loo, aren't we," groaned Lamp.

"I think so." Casper found the real light switch this time, flooding the tiny cubicle with its dazzling harshness. Now he saw the source of his wetness; his left foot was standing in the toilet-brush holder.

Daisy coughed and held her nose. "So this is what boys' toilets are like."

"They're not always this busy," said Lamp, removing his elbow from the sink. "Actually, Casper, why are we in here?"

"The front door's locked, but we can climb out of this window to get to Anemonie's house," said Casper.

Daisy frowned. "Why?"

"Look, the Blights aren't here and neither is Cuddles, but *everyone else* is! Nobody would dare to leave Cuddles alone in their house, so it has to be them. Either the Bluff Boiler got it wrong, or somehow they tricked us because one of them has to be *Le Chat*."

Lamp wasn't listening; he was dancing the funky chicken, despite the lack of music or elbow space.

"There's only one thing for it," came the muffled voice of Casper from somewhere near Lamp's armpit. "We need to go and catch them in the act."

Daisy's jaw dropped (which was a bad idea because it was instantly stuffed with feathers). "What, go right now?"

"But I'm doing dancing," moaned Lamp.

"I can see that."

"Shouldn't we just tell everyone?" Daisy looked worried.

"No, it has to be us. Adults are useless – Anemonie would spot them and hide Cuddles before we even made it to the front door."

"Then maybe we should wait until morning."

"Daisy, what's going on? I thought you wanted to catch *Le Chat*?"

"Yeah," she picked at a seam on her dress. "I'm just… nervous."

"Look, I'll go. You two have fun."

"OK." Lamp snatched Daisy's hand and flipped open the cubicle lock. "Come on, Daisy."

"Wait." Daisy yanked Lamp back before he could open the door. "We'll all go."

Casper was getting frustrated. "But you didn't want to come."

"I just think we should stick together, that's all."

Lamp murmured, "Yeah, that's all," and gripped Daisy's hand tighter.

"OK, come if you want, but we have to go now." Casper reached up to the small square window above the toilet and prised it open, taking a grateful gasp as the cool air rushed in to relieve his poor nostrils. Then with a leg up from the toilet-roll holder and both hands grabbing the cistern, he clambered into the window frame and squeezed through. He dropped, hands first, to the jagged gravel car park outside. "It's fine," he rasped, rubbing his stinging palms on the back of his jeans. "Just watch for the fall." *These window exits are fast becoming a hobby*, Casper thought.

Daisy swung through nimbly, legs leading the way, and landed softly on her feet. Then Lamp tumbled out, flapping his wings furiously, but crashing straight to the ground. "I'ng shtill learning," he muttered, munching a mouthful of gravel.

The strained sounds of Terry's bellowing wafted from the hall behind, but ahead there was only silence.

## Chapter 13

# Blight Manor

This chapter contains a long and little-known verb – to 'antiprofrogniloficate'. The definition of this word is – *To run the length of the landing, discover a door, but find that it is locked, then hear your baby sister through that door so try to open it, but fail, then bash on the door, but find that it just won't budge, then finally take a running jump at said door and kick it with all your might, at last succeeding in opening it, only to find your baby sister on the other side cuddling a cat.*

You probably won't have encountered this

word before unless you have a baby sister who likes locked rooms and cats, or if you read the dictionary in your spare time. There are only about six opportunities in the world ever to use 'antiprofrogniloficate' correctly, but this chapter is one of them. It's probably useful for you to know this before any antiprofrognilofication takes place and you get confused.

"We don't have to do this, you know." Daisy glanced back at the safety of the village hall.

"Yes, we do," said Casper, defiant. "Because if we don't, I'll lose Cuddles and my dad'll never get a new restaurant. I'm catching *Le Chat* if it's the last thing I do." He strode ahead of the others, feeling manly and powerful and wishing he had some sort of staff to thrash about.

The village was deserted now, apart from a

few forgotten detectives (including an old man in shorts) huddled together under a doorway in front of a small notebook bonfire. Casper led the way round the corner and up Long Lost Drive. He hadn't a clue what might await him at the end of the road, but he was ready – ready to get Cuddles back, and the sword and then the reward and his dad's restaurant and his mum's appreciation and Daisy's love and— Casper's stomach reared up and strangled his brain, making his eyes go all fizzy. What had just happened?

"No," he shook his head, "I can't think about that right now." He turned round and noticed that Lamp was watching her too. She dawdled behind them, eyes fixed on her own feet. Casper's heart beat faster so he turned back again and walked forward purposefully. Never had he come across

217

anyone like Daisy before; he understood her less than he understood ancient Greek. She was a girl, but he wanted to spend time with her. She was funny, she wore nice frocks, she even liked coming on adventures. But why the sudden change of heart – what was making her so nervous?

A chill grabbed the air and wrestled away its warmth as the road filtered away into a gravel path, and imposing blackened trees blotted out the dying sun, casting the three into darkness. Instantly Blight Manor reared up out of the night like an ugly vampire.

Lamp shivered. "This place gives me the wiggles."

"Come on," whispered Casper as he hurried away from the gravel path, under the cover of the trees. "They won't see us coming this way." He scuttled on into the shadows, eyes pinned to the windows for lookouts. The crumbly mansion loomed ever closer, but it looked empty – no light shone from the windows, no noise floated on the breeze.

"They're not even there," said Daisy. "Let's go back."

"They must be there."

"But what if they're not?"

"Then we…" Casper flailed about for an answer. "I don't know."

"Oof." Lamp tripped on a root and crashed to the ground, shaking a family of dozy jackdaws from the tree. They took to the air, croaking grumpily. Then a light was switched on and a pointy face poked from behind the curtains.

"It's Anemonie." Casper grabbed Daisy and leapt behind the tree.

Lamp lay still on the ground, doing his best impression of a feathery stone (receiving a score of nine from a nearby badger, nine point five from a woodlouse, but only four from the dozy jackdaws, giving a respectable average of seven point five).

Casper pressed himself to the tree, listening to Daisy's low and steady breathing as the light shone from Anemonie's window. Eventually the jackdaws stopped croaking and went back to bed, the light was turned off again and Anemonie retreated from the window.

"There's your answer, Daisy," said Casper, "and now we know where to find her."

"Do we?" said Lamp, so proud of his score that he hadn't noticed Anemonie.

"Guys, can't we just go back? I'm cold," said Daisy.

"But we're almost there," said Casper. "It'll be warmer inside."

They padded forward until the tree line ended, before dashing to the darkest corner of the house and pressing themselves flat against the wall. To Casper's left, the board covering a smashed window had warped away from the wall, leaving a large-enough gap to squeeze through. Casper grinned. "Well, it would be a window."

"No chance you're squeezing through there," said Daisy. "Let's come back tomorrow night with a crowbar. I know there's one in our shed."

"Daisy, I'm going in now. Come with me if you want; otherwise go home."

"Fine," she recoiled sharply. "I'll come."

Casper suddenly felt awful. That had come out much ruder than he meant it to. He looked round to apologise, but Daisy was facing the other way. "Come on, Casper, on with the task," he told himself. "Think about Daisy another time, maybe when you're not breaking into someone's house." Mouth pressed shut, praying for silence, he picked his way in, avoiding the shards of broken glass. Then he opened the frame from the inside for the other two. Lamp galumphed over the ledge, dusted himself off and grinned.

"We're in."

Blight Manor used to be the grandest, most beautiful house in the Kobb Valley, but those days were long gone. Centimetres of grot now covered the floor in a mucky grey rug of dead skin and beetles, while cobwebs hung off older cobwebs that dangled limply from more cobwebs like blocks of flats for spiders. There were probably rats about too, thought Casper, judging by the holes gnawed in the skirting boards and the rat sitting on Lamp's shoulder.

"I've made a friend," said Lamp. "His name's called Albert."

Albert nibbled on a feather.

"Shh," whispered Casper.

Albert nibbled a little more quietly.

Up the dusty staircase Casper crept, taking each step with the utmost care, watching out for creaky bits. Haughty portraits of the Blights' ancestors watched over him from the wall to his left: Lord Digby Blight wielding his bloodied sword and the head of an antelope; Lord Horatio Blight wielding his bloodied musket and the head of a wild boar; and a young Lord Tobias Blight wielding his smoking shotgun and the Head of Maths (recently retired).

What
a vile family
those Blights were, each more
evil than the last, each cutting a gaunt, skeletal
figure, smiling smarmily from under that
infamous pointy nose.

The staircase led to a marble landing, slightly
cleaner than downstairs, with delicate footprints

smudged in the
dust. Casper peered with
disgust into the dank and dingy rooms
passing on his left. A bathroom with a chipped sink
and the wrong half of a bath; a library scattered
with yellowed pages torn from books with cracked
spines; one room furnished only with a three-
and-a-half-poster, wrought-iron bed with rusty
springs poking through the mattress, a one-legged
wardrobe and a bare hanging light bulb.

"This must be where Anemonie sleeps,"
whispered Casper. "Imagine living here. No

wonder she's so grumpy."

Lamp patted his own shoulder and gasped. "Albert? He's gone! Daisy, have you seen—" Lamp swivelled round the room with panic in his eyes. "Daisy? She's gone! Casper, have you seen—" He spun back round and gave a sigh of relief. "Well, thank goodness you're still here."

"Actually, where is Daisy?" Casper's skin prickled, as if something was terribly wrong, but instantly it faded. "She'll catch up. Probably looking downstairs." He continued up the next flight of stairs, tailed by Lamp, who kept looking over his shoulder.

"Hope she's all right," whispered Lamp.

"She'll be fine."

"Because she was quite scared and I—"

"Shh, listen."

There was a noise from the far end of the second landing, like gurgling and then a *meow*.

"I know that noise…"

There was more gurgling, clearer this time, and a gnashing of teeth.

Then, for the first and last time in his life and without any word of a warning, Casper antiprofrogniloficated.

"Cuddles!" Casper cheered. "And Tiddles!"

Cuddles gurgled happily and squeezed Tiddles a little harder, which made the poor cat's eyes bulge.

"We've found you!" He ran forward to pick Cuddles up,

but she snarled at Casper's hand and shuffled backwards, Tiddles still clutched in her arms.

"Thank goodness for that," said Lamp. "D'you think Cuddles likes discos?"

"No, Lamp, we can't go back. This is all the proof we need that Anemonie is *Le Chat*. We've got to find her right now."

"Not if I find you first," snickered a sickly sweet voice in the doorway.

There was no time to look round. The next moment Casper felt a dull thud on the back of his head as the cricket bat struck home, and everything went black.

## Chapter 14

# The Cat

The first thing Casper noticed was the throbbing in his head much like a thumb under a hammer. The second thing was that he couldn't rub it because he couldn't budge his arms. Dizziness clouded his brain and swamped his memory. "Wh-where am I?"

"Stupid boy. You shouldn't have come here."

"Who's that? Mrs Blight?" The back of Casper's head pounded as if it was about to split. He could feel it swelling. "Ohh, that throbs."

A different voice spoke this time. "I told you not to come."

Shaking the buzz from his head, Casper tried to blink his swimming surroundings into focus. The room was dark and spinning round and there were at least two of everything. He was bound to his chair with thick rope. Two people stood before him: one woman, one girl. Or was it four? The shadows were playing tricks on Casper's dizzy eyes.

"Where am I? Where's Cuddles?"

"Cuddles is… gone."

Casper caught his breath. "Gone? As in—"

"She escaped," said the girl.

*Good on her*, thought Casper. No such luck for him, though – his ropes held fast.

Close to Casper's right ear, Lamp groaned snoozily.

"Lamp!" He'd never been so happy to hear his

friend in pain. "Are you OK?"

"Just five more minutes, Mum," he mumbled, and then let out a deep snore.

A mournful *meow* rose from Casper's left.

"Tiddles?"

*Meow*. The ropes tugged round Casper's chest. The three of them were tied up together in a circle.

"Let us go. We've done you no harm."

"Oh, what a good idea, let's untie you so you can tell the whole village about us," the woman in the dark cooed sarcastically. "Too bad you're not a bit brighter, Casper."

The moonlight appeared from behind a cloud, casting a silver glow on the faces of Lobelia Blight and her daughter Anemonie.

"Blights," spat Casper. "I *knew* it was you. Let me go *right now*."

Anemonie sniggered coldly. "You still think it was us?"

"Course I do. Cuddles was in your house. You just hit me over the head. You're standing right there, for goodness' sake. Who else could it be?"

"Things aren't always as they appear, Candlewacks," scorned Lobelia, wrinkling her nose hatefully.

"Just tell me this, Mrs Blight. How did you lie to the Bluff Boiler and get away with it?"

"How thick can you be, Candlewacks? I didn't lie."

Casper's brain pounded on the inside of his head like a slimy caged gorilla. Nothing was making any sense, and his double vision still wasn't fading.

"She didn't lie, Casper." A woman's voice, but not Lobelia's.

"Who's that? Somebody tell me what's going on!"

"And I thought you were clever. Ah well…" A second woman in a skin-tight black cat suit stepped forward into the patch of soft moonlight. She pulled back the black-eared hood, revealing her curly brown hair, her bright green eyes…

"Mrs Blossom!" Casper choked. "And that means…"

"Sorry, Casper," said Daisy, joining the other three in the moonlight. She'd also changed into a black leotard.

"You're *Le Chat*?"

Lavender Blossom rolled up a sleeve to reveal the so-called Venus Flytrap bites. "Guilty," she sang. "Your sister's a real biter."

"Wh-why?"

"Why not?" soothed Lavender. "It's our job. And, well…"

"Don't you dare," scorned Mrs Blight.

"Shut up, Lobelia. I can say what I want."

Casper's brain was still spinning. Questions without answers swirled about his head like a tornado of confusion spilling out of his ears and making the back of his neck tingle and his head throb even more. "Wait, you know each other?"

"You could say that," Lavender smiled gracefully. "We're sisters."

Casper caught his breath. "No…" But the more he looked at Lavender's face next to Lobelia's, the more he saw what he hadn't before. Keen eyes, angular face, and that nose. How hadn't he noticed? Lavender's nose was pointy. Not poke-out-your-eyes pointy like the Blights'. But it was there – elegant, yes, but *pointy*. "So… Anemonie and Daisy are…"

"Cousins, yes. Small world."

"Bit too small," Anemonie grunted.

"The dolphins are coming, we're saved!" Lamp cried, bursting from his dream with triumph. "Oh." He tugged on his ropes (making Tiddles wheeze like a bagpipe), and then spotted the two Blossoms by the window. "Hey, Daisy, it's me. Lamp. Can you untie me?"

Daisy turned away and covered her face, barely muffling a sob.

Lavender clicked her teeth. "Oh, grow up, you pitiful girl. It's your fault for getting involved with them."

"What's going on?" Lamp's voice wavered.

"How stupid can you be?" spat Anemonie. "They stole the sword and now they're setting us up."

"Not Daisy. Daisy wouldn't do that."

"Poor little Lampy. Never suspects his girlfriend."

"No," Lamp sniffed. "No, it's not true. Tell her, Daisy."

A sob floated from the corner.

Lamp fell silent.

Casper felt something on the left side of his face and smiled. Tiddles was licking his cheek. "Thanks, boy. Sorry we got you into this."

Tiddles purred.

But wait… something else was wrong. A memory blundered its way forward through the ache in Casper's head and sat there, blinking at him. Their last meeting with Tiddles, that time in the greenhouse. What had he missed? Bad balance, clumsiness, this licking didn't really tickle at all…

Casper gasped.

"I can't feel his whiskers. Tiddles doesn't have any whiskers. You took them!"

"Well," Lavender extended her arms in apology. "We needed to sign our notes with something."

"That's evil. You're evil." Casper felt sick, but he pushed on, his mind still riddled with questions. "What about your arms, Anemonie? You had bites too. We saw them."

Lavender laughed silently. "Oh, Casper, you really don't get it. While I've been babynapping, they've been baby*sitting*."

"So they're in on it too?"

"Oh, no, no," she said, laughing. "We don't get on, them and us. I'm afraid we had to be a little… stronger in our methods."

"What do you mean?"

"Ever heard of blackmail, Casper?" Retreating

to the far corner of the room, Lavender picked up a small collection of items. "Right then, girls, over here. Now, same rules apply. Try anything clever and I tell the villagers. Understood?"

Anemonie hissed.

"I'll take that as a 'yes'." Lavender smirked as Anemonie snatched the items from her – a cricket bat, a pot of glue and a bulging brown paper bag. "Let's get to work."

Lavender stood watching over the operation while Lobelia dabbed glue on to the blade of the bat. Anemonie pulled from the paper bag a blood-red jelly bean and stuck it down.

"Those belong to Betty Woons!" Casper yelled. "You stole them too."

"Naturally," chortled Lavender.

"Um," It was Daisy, standing sulkily in front of

the boys. "I owe you an apology."

"Bit late for that," snarled Casper. "You tricked us."

"I'm not talking to you any more, Daisy," said Lamp. "Except for that bit. And that bit."

"You should've listened to me. You could be at the ball right now, not tied up here."

"Then let us go."

"And that bit."

"It's not that easy."

"Why not?"

"Let me explain."

## Chapter 15

# The Cat's Tale

"There're a lot of things I haven't told you about who I am. Who I *really am*, I mean." Daisy spoke in hushed tones so that the others couldn't hear. "Maybe at the end you'll forgive me a bit. I hope so."

"Doubt it," said Casper.

"Well, it'll make me feel better, anyway."

Casper didn't reply, so she began. "I guess it starts with my mum. Her surname's not really 'Blossom'. She was born Lavender Potatia Blight, first child to Lord and Lady Benson Blight, the wealthiest couple in the Kobb Valley. My granddad wanted a son as an heir so he demanded that Mum become a boy. Of course she couldn't, so Granddad never spoke to her again. Grandma thought children were a bore so she only visited the nursery wing of the house when she drank too much gin and forgot the way back to her room.

"When Mum was four my grandparents had a second daughter, Lobelia Tomatia Blight. She wasn't a boy either, so Granddad threw rotten fruit at her. Grandma tried to sell them at a jumble sale, but they hid in a box of cutlery and nobody bought them.

"Mum says Lobelia was a pale, sickly girl who only went outside during thunderstorms. Looking at her now I can see she was right. She was afraid of daylight and noise; apparently her only friends were the spiders in the attic.

Worst of all, she absolutely hated Mum – mostly because she was first in line to inherit the Blight fortune. Jealous, that's what she was. It wasn't as if Mum was going to inherit a thing anyway – Granddad set out to spend every penny of the fortune before his daughter could get it. Mum says he'd wash his feet in baths of vintage champagne, crush up diamonds on his cornflakes and roll his sports cars off cliffs when they ran out of petrol.

"When she was sixteen, Mum got wind of the fact that their parents were going to sneak off to a cottage in the Scottish highlands without them, so she and Lobelia stowed away in the car boot. She got her holiday, but she'd pay for it. In a game of hide-and-seek on their final day, Mum went into the cellar and hid behind a barrel. Lobelia spotted her opportunity, jumped in the car with Grandma and Granddad and drove home without her.

"They forgot about Mum. She roamed the highlands for six months, sleeping in barns and stealing food through kitchen windows. Mum doesn't tell me much about this part because she says she's ashamed, but what I do know is that she ended up meeting someone called Tamworth Ringshank, a gypsy pickpocket with one eye and eleven fingers. He stole her heart and he stole her wallet, and they were married within a week.

He taught mum every trick in the pickpocket's book as they travelled the world in his caravan. He even taught her how to steal the pickpocket's book. Mum was happy for the first time in her life. She changed her name, cut her hair… she even managed to forget about the Blights.

"He's my dad, this Tamworth guy. I never met him, though… The moment Mum told him I was on the way he got spooked and scarpered.

"So I grew up on the move. I've never lived in one place for longer than a month. As soon as I could walk, Mum was teaching me the pickpocket's way. I stole my first dummy from the mouth of Princess Tabitha the Third. I've never paid for a meal in my life. I'd have nicked your wallets if either of you ever carried one.

"Oy," said Casper.

"It's the truth," said Daisy. "It's the only way I've ever known. At least I'm being honest with you now."

Casper grunted.

"So this is my life. Mum and me, we steal stuff. I can't pretend we don't. Every time the police almost catch up with us, we change our disguise and move on. *Le Chat* was my idea, actually. Mum says it's 'too flamboyant'. I think it's pretty cool.

"We happened to be travelling through the Kobb Valley when Mum decided to steal the sword. What with the Blights living here, we had a bit of power. If they didn't do what we wanted, Mum could just stride in and claim Blight Manor for her own. Not that she actually wants a big house like that – she's spent too many years on the open road to settle down now. It's more of a bargaining chip.

"Anyway, we like to get a good picture of an area before we steal from it, so that's why we set up our flower shop here. Quite quickly we realised that the village wasn't much of a threat."

"Oh. Thanks."

"Apart from you two! I spotted you were different immediately. That's why Mum made me… um… say hi to you back at the garage."

"That's why you made friends with us? To spy on us?"

"Sorry. Yeah."

"Unbelievable."

"But it's not just that, Casper. I'm glad I met you two. I *like* you. It's such a shame we had to meet like this. We could've been friends."

"Yeah. It is a shame you're a liar and a thief."

"Well, we're leaving Corne-on-the-Kobb in a

247

minute, and I can never come back. You won't have to worry about me again. Onwards and upwards, I s'pose…" Daisy's words trailed off and she was left standing there foolishly.

"What are you doing over there, girl? Stop faffing and make yourself useful." Lavender waved dismissively and Daisy shuffled off into the corner to pack some things.

Lobelia Blight scowled her stony face as she dabbed more glue on the bat. Almost all of the jelly beans were now in place. "Do you suppose it'll fool them?"

Lavender uncovered Sir Gossamer's gleaming bejewelled sword from beneath a black cloth and held it beside the be-jellybeaned cricket bat, her head cocked on one side. "Of course it will. They're a pack of idiots."

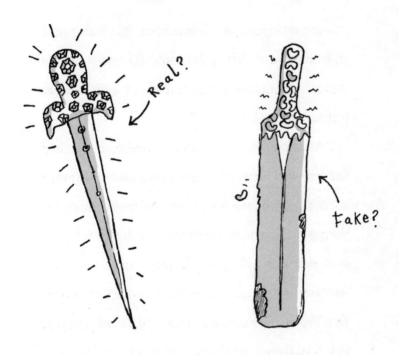

Real?

Fake?

Anger churned up through Casper's chest like boiling bile and coursed through his veins, prickling and tensing.

Lamp snuffled beside Casper, his feathers all droopy and grey. "S'not fair."

Casper longed to burst from his ropes and grab the sword, but all he could do was watch as those wicked Blossoms went about their wicked business.

"Ah, finished." Lavender smiled and snatched the counterfeit sword from Lobelia, inspecting it closely beneath the moonlight. "Very good, girls." Wrapping it in a second black cloth she returned it to Anemonie. "Now, pip pip, time to get you into your cat cozzies. You'll need to look just like *Le Chat* if the villagers are going to believe it *is* you. And once you've been caught red-handed, we'll go free! Now don't try anything clever." She flashed her savage green eyes and ushered the Blights out of the room, following behind with the genuine sword. "Oh, do hurry up, Daisy. You're being pathetic."

Daisy shuffled from the shadows, her eyes bleary and red, lower lip wobbling. She turned to Casper and Lamp and just blinked. With a sob, she dashed from the room after her mother, clopping down the stairs and into the darkness.

The only sounds after that were the boys' breathing and the occasional low moan from Tiddles. Nothing moved, nothing happened.

Eventually Casper sighed. "Well, that's that then."

"If only I could just reach my rope cutters," said Lamp.

"Where are they?"

"In the garage."

"Oh."

"Bit far."

"Yeah."

"Sorry."

"It's all right."

"Game of I-Spy?"

"Not now, Lamp."

"S'pose we've got time for that later."

Nothing happened. Casper's head throbbed rhythmically, buzzing in his ears once a second. A dozy jackdaw croaked past the window, flapping its wings victoriously. The house creaked and groaned under the weight of unseen shadows and the ghosts of long-dead Blights, but still nothing happened.

I mean, things happened, yes. But nothing important did, anyway. Basically, it was really boring and went on for ages so we might as well skip Chapter 16 and go straight to the important bit.

## Chapter 17

# The Important Bit

The rough rope dug into Casper's wrists and burnt the skin. "Oh, I'll go bonkers if we're stuck here for any longer. Got any ideas?"

"Hmmm." You could tell Lamp was concentrating when his head made grinding noises. "Skiing?"

"How would that help?"

"Can't remember. Albert, got any ideas?"

Albert squeaked.

Tiddles meowed.

Something downstairs scrabbled.

Casper gasped. "What was that downstairs? Was it Cuddles?"

"I dunno," said Lamp. "I'll ask Albert. Albert, did you hear anything?"

Albert squeaked.

Tiddles meowed.

The thing downstairs scrabbled again.

"It must be Cuddles. She can hear Tiddles! Ask Alb— Hang on. Who's Albert?"

"He's my rat, remember?" chuckled Lamp. "He's on my head again. I think he likes the feathers."

"But this is brilliant! Keep asking him questions."

"OK. Erm, so, Albert, where did you go on your

254

holidays last year?"

Albert squeaked.

Tiddles let out a desperate *meow* and clawed at his ropes.

The scrabbling turned into scribbling.

"Perfect! Keep going." Casper bit his lip.

"Don't s'pose they let you on an aeroplane. Did you take the bus?"

Another squeak, and Tiddles *meow*ed savagely.

The scribbling became scrobbling, and soon increased to scrubbling (which is the best of all of them).

"How much do bus tickets cost for rats, anyway?"

Every squeak made Tiddles more excited. He wriggled and snapped, *meow*ing as loud as his feline throat would allow.

"Come on!" shouted Casper. "Come on!"

The scrubbling was coming from right outside the door now. The three captives and Albert fell silent.

There was a snarl and a yap, then the door went *BAM* as it flew off its hinges. In its wake floated a cloud of dust bathed in the evening's moonlight; within the cloud a tiny silhouette stood rigid. The dust slowly settled. There she stood – a raggedy toddler in a tattered pink all-in-one with chalk-white hair and a mouthful of spoons that she must've found in the Blights' cutlery drawer.

"Cuddles!" Casper almost toppled his chair in excitement.

At once Cuddles spotted Tiddles and her mouth fell open, the forgotten spoons clattering to the floor. "TATATA!" she screeched, bounding across

256

the room in graceful leaps. She leapt on to Tiddles' chair with bared teeth, licked him once on the nose and then set to work gnawing the ropes.

"Good, Cuddles, you keep biting." Casper's heart beat faster as he felt the bonds fraying and loosening. "Come on, come on…"

With a last gnash and a screech of delight, Cuddles snapped through the bonds and grabbed Tiddles, squeezing him like a ketchup bottle and licking his ear.

"Yes!" Casper pulled away the loose ropes and jumped free. Lamp followed, stretching and shaking his creaky bits.

"I love you so much, you little monster!" Casper fed Cuddles the last doggy treat from his pocket and ruffled her nit-ridden hair.

She snapped at Casper's finger, then belly-flopped off the chair, her landing cushioned by Tiddles clutched tightly to her chest.

"Casper, Casper," Lamp hopped from foot to foot. "What about the sword?"

"Oh, blimey, I almost forgot. There's still a chance we'll catch them if we hurry. You ready to run, Lamp?"

Lamp's shoulders sagged. "Can't I just invent something?"

"There's no time. We have to go." He lumped Cuddles and Tiddles into his arms and set off down the corridor. Lamp blundered behind him holding Albert firmly on his head like an oddly fitting hat.

They were down the stairs and out of the door in no time, dashing from the house along the crisp gravel path that twisted into Long Lost Drive and curved round the neat row of houses before dumping them back in the village square. The big clock read half past eleven, but the party still raged on inside the hall and showed no signs of abating. Left and across the park would lead them past Lamp's garage and out towards Upper Crustenbury, but just as they reached 'Blossom's Bloomers' a horrible thought slapped Casper round the face like a soggy haddock.

He stopped suddenly and grabbed Lamp's arm. "There are two roads out of the village. Which one did they take?"

Lamp shrugged. "Don't ask me. I was tied up in a mansion."

"But they could be miles away if we don't get a move on!"

"Never heard of 'miles away'. Is it near Upper Crustybelly?"

There was no time to think. Casper flung Cuddles and Tiddles into Lamp's arms. "Go, quickly. Take the south road past your house. We can't let them get away!"

"But what do I do when I find them?" asked Lamp. "I don't think I'm very good at stopping robbers."

"Just use Cuddles. Lavender's dressed as a cat, remember?"

"TAT?" Cuddles' ears pricked up.

"Exactly. At the sight of Lavender, let her rip. Now run!"

"Run, run, run," repeated Lamp as he gallumphed off towards the park with Cuddles and Tiddles and Albert as a hat.

Casper spun on his heels and headed back through the square. The Blossoms could be long gone by now, but it was worth a try.

There are only two ways out of Corne-on-the-Kobb: one road to the north and one to the south. The hills to the east house a pack of wolves so savage that the sheep carry shotguns. West of the village runs the River Kobb, but all the bridges collapsed during National Bridge-Stamping Day four years ago, and nobody rebuilt them thanks to International Bridge-Blueprint-Ripping-Up Day, which took place a week later. Leaving Corne-on-the-Kobb downwards would pose problems without Lamp's Solar-Spade, and going up's not easy when you don't have wings or a hot-air balloon to hand. So there really were only two ways for the Blossoms to escape Corne-on-the-Kobb, and the northern one of those ways was currently being raced along by Casper Candlewacks.

Casper panted in time with his footsteps, sucking in the cool air and pushing himself forward. The school slipped by on the left, the church on the right and then he was running down a wide road flanked by high hedgerows. Somewhere along this road was the burly guard Baz Laszlo, Corne-on-the-Kobb's joint strongest man (a title he's shared with his brother, Gaz, for the last twelve years because they couldn't bear to hit each other in the final punch-up). Baz had biceps the size of ostrich eggs, but a brain the size of a walnut. The Blossoms might not last twelve rounds against this hulk, but they could easily outwit him with some craftily placed mirrors or a rubber mouse on a string.

A light flickered in the distance. Surely that was Baz's checkpoint? Casper picked up pace, willing his legs to carry him faster, gasping for air. Then

something glinted in the darkness and Casper dived to the ground, breathing hard. He squinted into the pitch-black night and… yes! Between him and the flickering light were two cat-shaped creatures creeping under the shadow of the hedgerow. "The Blossoms," he breathed, "or is it the Blights?" The shapes crept ever forward. But something was wrong – they'd be caught for sure. How were they going to get past Baz?

*Maybe it's an ambush.* Casper glanced around for the others, but they were nowhere to be seen. He scratched his head frantically. *Think, you idiot, think.* But nothing useful got thought.

"Oy!" The shout came from the perfectly toned throat of Baz Laszlo. He'd spotted them. "Who's that?"

Casper edged closer. Who were they?

In a flash Baz leapt from his checkpoint and grabbed the figures, lifting them by the ears of their black cat suits back into the light.

A spring of joy filled Casper's heart. Baz had caught the Blossoms!

"It's you two. And what's this…" He pulled the sparkling bejewelled sword from its cloth and choked on his own muscly tongue. "Oh my gawd…" Baz fumbled with a walkie-talkie. "'Ere, Gaz," he shouted. "Gaz, you there? Over."

There was a crackle and then, "Wossup? Over."

"I got *Le Chat*, don't I! Get 'ere now, and bring the mayor over. Over."

"Wicked, bruv. Who was it? Over."

"It's those Blights, innit. Over."

"All right, I'm comin' over. Over and out."

Casper went pale. The Blights? But they were

only carrying the *fake* sword. The decoy had worked. Without thinking he bounded from his hiding place. "It's not them!"

Baz, Anemonie and Lobelia all jumped.

"What d'you fink you're up to?" shouted Baz.

"Listen to me, that sword's a fake."

"Shut it, I'd recognise the sword anywhere. You just want the cash."

"You have to believe me. That's a decoy. Tell Gaz to get back to his post!"

"Whatever. You're just jealous."

"Run, Candlewacks," Anemonie rasped, wrinkling her pointy nose. "Run."

There was no time to lose. Casper hurtled back towards the village faster than the opposite of a tortoise. With Gaz not guarding his checkpoint, the Blossoms had a free route out of the village, and who knows how far Lamp and Cuddles had got. Knowing Lamp, he'd probably forgotten about the whole thing and gone to bed. The church blurred by, then the school, then the square where bewildered idiots with party hats were piling out of the hall at Gaz's frantic command.

"It's a trick!" Casper yelled. "You've got to come with me."

"Who's got my sword?" Audrey Snugglepuss rolled up her sleeves menacingly.

"LET ME AT HER!" bellowed Mayor Rattsbulge, his flabby bloodhound cheeks swollen with rage.

"This way," shouted Gaz, "foller me."

"The sword's mine!"

"Not if I get there first."

"You're going the wrong way! Listen to me –

that sword's a fake. *Le Chat*'s escaping!" Casper's yells fell on deaf ears as the herd thundered away from him, walking sticks and knitting needles thrashing around. Gaz Laszlo flung Clemmie Answorth out of his path and she flew off into the night, landing, bewildered, in a nearby field.

"Ugh," Casper hopped with desperation. "There's no time for this." He took a despairing look at the idiots and then launched himself in the other direction. Blossom's Bloomers sat empty, moonlight reflecting off its spotless front window. It billowed its green awning rather proudly as Casper raced past. The scene in front of him pitched and reeled like he was on a boat; his lungs burned, his legs ached, only his mind pushed him on.

Bring home Cuddles, plus twenty thousand

pounds and life would finally return to normal. Bring home nothing and who knows if he'd ever get his parents off that sofa? What if Lamp hadn't got there in time? What if they'd snatched Cuddles again? They could be miles away by now.

Sweat stung Casper's eyes as he passed Lamp's garage – empty, thank goodness.

"I'm coming for you, Lavender Blossom," Casper yelled into the sky. "You're not getting away with this."

The trees blocked the moonlight, casting the road into darkness. How much further? Casper's arms had dropped, his shirt was clinging to his skin, he couldn't gasp enough air with each breath, but he pressed on ever further into the darkness.

Suddenly a light up ahead shook Casper back into focus. Gaz's checkpoint. No movement. He

willed his numb legs to sprint the last fifty metres and arrived, wheezing, to find… nothing.

The place was deserted. An overturned chair lay next to Gaz's torch in a ditch at the side of the road, which was illuminating the hedgerows above rather prettily, given the situation. Casper doubled over with hands on knees, downcast and exhausted. Beyond the checkpoint was a fork in the road where both choices trailed off into blackness. There was no sign of Lamp or Cuddles, no clue as to where the Blossoms had gone; nothing at all. Silence closed in on Casper's ears and hugged him like a muffly bear.

"Where are you?" He strutted forward furiously and kicked a little clod of earth. Except that it wasn't earth because it sort of disintegrated under his feet. More like… a clump of hair. Casper crouched down and picked some up – it was soft to the touch, curly too and quite fragrant. He stood up again and moved forward, eyes to the ground. There was more – another whole clump, trailing off towards the left-hand fork. "Hang on," Casper's eyes widened. "*Curly…*"

Adrenalin surged back through Casper's body as he raced down the left road, hot on his new trail. That hair was unmistakeably Lavender or Daisy Blossom's. So what had happened? More clumps of the hair were strewn on the road every few metres with no real pattern. Round the next corner was a crushed sweet pea, then a shred of purple sparkly material. There was only one possible explanation for such carnage – *Cuddles*. Casper lifted his head now, not looking for hair, but for people on the road. Only the thought of Cuddles round every corner could possibly spur him any further onwards.

Just as he felt he could go no further, Casper's eyes made out a wriggling shape against the blackness, accompanied by a series of grunts. It was large, bumpy and it squirmed. Grinding to a halt about twenty metres away, he gulped two lungfuls of delicious air and squinted at the shape.

"Who's that?"

"Casper! Help!"

As Casper limped forward, the moon advanced from behind a cloud and filled in the scene before his eyes. There stood Lavender, staggering about blindly and thrashing the sword from side to side while Cuddles lay on top of her head and hugged her face, both sets of claws dug firmly into her chin. Meanwhile Lamp clung desperately round

Lavender's legs and Tiddles climbed up and down her body, nipping at any bits of bare skin.

"Get off me, you vile beasts!" she yelled, screeching and wobbling and waving her sword.

"TATATA!" yelled Cuddles.

"Grab the sword!" shouted Lamp. "I can't hold on much longer."

Casper approached Lavender, ducking her swishes of the sword and the flecks of her enraged spit. With Cuddles cuddling Lavender's eyes, she was absolutely blind, but with Casper tired from all his running and the perfect height for decapitation, the duel was about evenly matched.

The bejewelled sword swished across the top of Casper's head and sent him reeling to one side and straight into a hedgerow. He winced at the pain, but there was no time to rest. Taking two deep breaths,

Casper gritted his teeth and launched back into the fray. He advanced on the crazed woman, keeping low this time to avoid the sword's wayward thrashes. Casper crouched right in front of her now, an arm's length from the sword. Lavender swung the blade from side to side far too fast to grab, but Casper noticed that between swishes, for a couple of seconds the sword was still. Could Casper take that chance to snatch it?

"I know you're there somewhere, Casper."

Swish, swish, swish.

If he popped up too early she'd take his head with her.

Swish, swish, swish.

"Quick, Casper. My arms hurt!"

Swish, swish, swish.

Between two swishes and by pure instinct Casper sprang to a standing position and in the same move wrenched the bejewelled sword from Lavender's grasp. She screamed and lunged forward, but Lamp tightened his grip on her ankles. With a muffled scream Lavender lost her balance, tumbled right over Casper in a gangly half-somersault and thumped on to her back on the warm tarmac. Winded and swordless, she didn't bother to get up again.

"We've got the sword! We've got the sword!" Lamp stood up and jigged about in front of Casper, then leapt forward to hug him and then pushed him away for another jig. Casper held the sword numbly, unable to move or speak or do sums (not that he needed to do any), filled with heavy, exhausted relief. Cuddles had sniffed out that Lavender was no cat by now and pinned her to the ground, angrily chewing on a mouthful of her hair.

The sword was theirs, Cuddles was safe and they'd brought Lavender Blossom to justice. Casper's heart swelled with happiness like only once ever before.

Lamp skipped in gleeful circles round Lavender. "Wheee! Just wait till I tell Alb— Oh."

"What?"

"Albert. I left him guarding Daisy."

Casper looked around, but he knew what he'd see, or rather what he wouldn't see. Daisy was long gone.

"She told me she surrendered. I believed her. So did Albert. We believed her, Casper. But now she's run away and she's taken Albert…" Lamp's face crumpled. He trumpeted into his hanky and emitted the mournful cries of "Albert! Daisy!"

Lavender spat a mouthful of dirt on to the road. "You'll never find her, you snivelling little infant. Should've caught her when you had the— AARGH!"

Cuddles and Tiddles had sunk their teeth into

each of Lavender's arms.

Casper didn't usually give hugs, but he was certain that Lamp needed one. "Come on," he said, lending his friend a comforting arm. "A girl like that would probably have been a whole lot of trouble anyway."

"S'pose so," muttered Lamp.

"You got the sword and you caught Lavender. That's two things worth celebrating."

Lamp sniffed, then smiled. "S'pose so."

Cuddles chuckled and tried to bend Lavender's arm the wrong way.

One mile away Julius and Amanda Candlewacks snored in tuneless harmony as *Nature's Curliest Tentacles* tickled their dreams.

Two miles away the pigeons fluttered down

from the rafters and hungrily pecked at Mayor Rattsbulge's abandoned sausage rolls.

Three miles away, Clemmie Answorth couldn't find her way home, so she stopped to ask for directions from a snarling wolf.

Four miles away, Mayor Rattsbulge picked a jellybean off the fake plastic sword and chewed slowly, confusion etched across his blubbery face.

Five miles away, a green-eyed, curly-haired young girl in a black leotard knocked on the wooden door of Mr and Mrs Higgins, claiming that her name was Poppy Bouquet and that she was lost. They invited her in warmly with the promise of hot chocolate and a bed. The next morning when they came to wake her she was gone, as were the contents of Mrs Higgins's jewellery drawer.

# Aftermath

The boys took one of Lavender's arms each while Cuddles perched on her head, claws dug deep into her scalp. Together they herded their prisoner back to Corne-on-the-Kobb, while Tiddles wound his way clumsily around their feet. Mayor Rattsbulge was delighted to see the sword, more delighted still when he couldn't eat the rubies, but then utterly undelighted when he had to fork out twenty thousand of his precious pounds to the mucky boys that stood before him. Baz and Gaz Laszlo dragged Lavender to the cellar of the Horse and Horse (to be dealt with in the morning) and triple-padlocked the trapdoor, while the Blights were released without an apology.

The crowds were furious that they hadn't got their reward and sneered over their spectacles at the boys. Cuddles hung round Casper's neck, lurching out to gnash villagers as they passed.

They stopped by the postbox on Feete Street and Casper counted two hundred crumpled fifty-pound notes out of the mayor's plastic bag of money and handed them to Lamp. "Ten thousand pounds. That's half."

He looked at the wad of cash for a while and then gave it back. "I don't really want it. Money's boring. Give my half to your dad."

"I was giving him my half too," grinned Casper.

"Can he buy a new restaurant with that much?"

"Hope so, I'm starving."

"Me too." Lamp rubbed his belly. "All I've had is eggs."

Cuddles yapped, so Casper gave her a fifty-pound note to chew on.

"Well, bye then, Casper," grinned Lamp. "I like it when we go on adventures."

"Yeah. Tiring though." Casper yawned.

"See you tomorrow?"

"Definitely."

Lamp sponged off down the road, leaving a wake of filthy feathers.

Amanda screamed when she saw Cuddles and spun her round in circles, smothering her in sloppy smooches until the scratching stung too much. The bag of money gave Julius a coughing fit, but he put on a serious face and told Casper, "We'll talk about this in the morning."

Bed felt comforting and homely. Casper

gingerly lowered his swollen skull to the pillow and winced, but soon the pain softened and his eyes drooped shut.

Three days had passed since the sword was recovered and everything had slipped back to normal. The morning after the ball a shiny new police car marked 'High Kobb Constabulary' had pulled up outside the Horse and Horse, and out had stepped a smart-suited copper with polished shoes. With the help of Mitch McMassive, he bundled Lavender Blossom into the back and sped away, leaving no trace but the smell of diesel fumes and a self-important grin on Mitch's tiny face.

Julius had spent the last three days tinkering away in his brand-new restaurant in the space left by Blossom's Bloomers, measuring gaps for ovens and sharpening his knives. Meanwhile across the square the funny little Frenchman was furnishing his own shop in the burnt-out plot where Julius's old restaurant had once stood (before the explosion). Julius didn't understand a word of French and the man, René, refused to speak in English, but they'd struck up an unlikely friendship anyway after Julius lent René a hammer. Now they'd sit in the square together during tea breaks, recounting stories in their own languages and laughing heartily.

Since Julius was as busy as he'd ever been, and Amanda was busy with Cuddles (and her three new fangs), Casper was free to spend the dying days of summer with Lamp.

"Caught anything yet?" Lamp lay on his belly, squinting into the cool water of the River Kobb.

"I don't think it's working." Casper wiggled the

rod, but it didn't feel any heavier.

"Maybe change the channel."

Casper prodded a button on the remote control taped to the reel and the little screen on the end of the line flicked from a soap opera to a football match. "This won't work, Lamp. Fish don't like football."

"Why not?"

"They don't have feet."

"Try another channel. Swimming or something."

Casper silently hopped through the channels, hoping a fish would come and take a seat soon before his arm dropped off.

"I miss Daisy," said Lamp.

"I know. Me too."

"And Albert. Where do you think they are now?" Lamp rolled on to his back and gazed into the sky.

"Monaco," said Casper, "stealing pearls from a princess's necklace."

"Or France," Lamp grinned, "grabbing paintings from a museum while the guards are having their sandwiches."

"Hijacking a boat and sailing to Venice."

"Jumping out of a plane on the run from the police."

Casper sighed, taking in the peace of the balmy summer afternoon.

"Casper?"

"Yes?"

Lamp scratched his sticky black hair. "Do you think love is some metaphysical phenomenon wholly irreducible to the mundanities of neuro-physiological explanations, or do you think it really can be accounted for solely by the mechanistic relational properties of the brain?"

Casper's mouth fell open. The rod slipped from his hands and plopped into the river. He stared at his friend. "What?"

"Oh, nothing."